a
SOCIAL ILLUSION

by

Jason T. Shapiro

TREE
MOUTH
BOOKS

Published by **TREE MOUTH Books**, an imprint of:

Peter Weisz Publishing, LLC

7143 Winding Bay Lane

West Palm Beach, FL 33412   USA

peter@peterweisz.com

Shapiro, Jason T., June, 2022

A Social Illusion / Jason T. Shapiro

Fiction — Biography — Nostalgia — Self-Help — Personal Improvement

ISBN: 9 781387 872008

Printed in the United States of America by Lulu.com.

1 2 3 4 5 6 7 8 9 10

Other books by Jason Shapiro:

The Magic of Mayfair

Brian, My Pet Lion

The Magnificent Mind of Ostaf

Lunch with Larry

A Social Illusion

Dedication

To my beautiful wife, Andrea:
I strive to make you proud.

To Alyssa and Ryan:

Thank you for being my toughest writing critics. You make me a better author.

A Social Illusion

Contents

Author's Preface 1

Foreword 3

Chapter One: Fakebook 5

Chapter Two: Behind the Filter...13

Chapter Three: Surf and Turf...21

Chapter Four: A Promotional Fantasy....................................25

Chapter Five: Family Heirlooms 31

Chapter Six: Blind Envy 37

Chapter Seven: Paid in Full 41

Chapter Eight: Brotherly Love..49

Chapter Nine: "Put Down Your Phone!" 55

Chapter Ten: A Blast From the Past......................................59

Chapter Eleven: Mall Therapy...71

Chapter Twelve: Turning the Corner 79

Chapter Thirteen: REDEMPTION 81

Chapter Fourteen: Diamonds Are Forever................................89

Chapter Fifteen: Swoosh! 95

Chapter Sixteen: Date Night 99

Chapter Seventeen: Awakening 105

Chapter Eighteen: A Social Reality......................................111

Epilogue 117

Acknowledgements..121

Special Thanks 123

About the Author..124

Author's Preface

From a distance, social media connects us in ways we never imagined. It offers us instant visibility to sentimental photographs and videos that often tug on our heartstrings. We're able to interact and build relationships without leaving our couch. We can instantly share the highlights of our lives and the moments we treasure.

I have become interested in the intricacies of social media. It's fascinating when you take the time to peek behind the curtain. An ecosystem exists that many are not aware of—a world that presents itself as euphoric and inviting, a place where we can escape and unwind.

But what lurks behind all the smiles and laughter...the joy and celebrations? Are things always as they seem? This question has intrigued me for years.

I wrote this book because I believe this story can benefit others. As social media continues to dominate our lives, it's crucial that we become mindful of how this powerful entity can impact our mental health.

When we are conscious of the reality we live in, we can take the necessary steps to improve our futures.

A Social Illusion

Foreword

by Eric Kussin

Founder and CEO of #SameHere–
The Global Mental Health Movement

Too often we go through life comparing ourselves—to others, to some artificial timeline we have made up that measures our "success," and to social norms. In this book, Jason Shapiro shines a light on the reality that we can only become our best selves, and feel grounded, when we stop comparing and start living life to the fullest, focusing on what makes us feel good, and not what makes us look good or helps us keep up with certain expectations that truly don't matter.

As someone who "found himself" as a writer only after he'd already established himself in another long and successful career, the theme of this book mirrors perfectly how Jason's life has played out. He's found purpose and meaning in the things that he's discovered matter most to him: helping others, being generous with his time, and using his literary talents to share themes that open up society to the realization that while we all struggle, there is beauty even in the struggle. When we are real about our hurdles, we can best heal, rise above the challenges we face, and be a beacon of hope to others.

Jason provides readers with a character facing a common dilemma so many of us face, and one that extends to many age groups: how we appear to others on social media and how often it becomes an unrealistic measure of our worth, especially as we try to project something we are not. This is a topic that hasn't been discussed nearly enough, given how recently and quickly technology has advanced.

Jason grew up in an era when sharing our lives was done through printed photos from trips, VHS tapes, and even slide shows. Now, seeing how much immediate and continuous digital comparisons have become a part of our lives, at such a rapid pace and with such ease, he was the perfect person, with the perfect perspective, to address this topic. He created characters that expose the challenges posed by modern society, and is himself a grounded enough individual to show through the power of storytelling how we can take back control over digital comparisons in our own lives. It's not often a book can be both entertaining and educational, and this one accomplishes both.

Chapter One

Fakebook

"Hello, Sir! Welcome to Dean De Carlo Mercedes-Benz. What may I help you with today?" The receptionist greets Trevor at the front desk. She leans forward and runs her fingers through her hair.

Trevor glances at her name badge and looks into her piercing blue eyes. "Hey, Sydnee. Is there someone in sales who can help me? I'm looking to buy a new car today." Trevor rocks back and forth on his heels and eyes the showroom inventory.

"Absolutely! Let me go grab Donnie. He'll take good care of you. Just so you're aware, our Winter Enchantment Promotion started this week." Sydnee points to the enormous banner that hangs from the showroom's open-ceiling rafters. "Donnie can tell you all about it. Oh, before I forget, can I have your name, please?"

"Sure. My name is Trevor Huxley."

Sydnee types his name into the guest log. "Huxley…Huxley… that name sounds familiar."

"Well, I went to West Mountain High and graduated in '94. My brother, Jordan, was class of '96." Trevor tries to recall if there's any other prior connection to the attractive receptionist.

Sydnee snaps her fingers and points into the air. "That's it! I knew your brother. I also went to West Mountain through my junior year. Then my parents divorced and I finished at Oak Park. I moved in with my dad my senior year. It's a long story. I won't bore you with the details."

"No problem. What a small world. I'll tell my brother I ran into you. What's your last name? I'll friend you on Facebook." Trevor is eager for a response.

Sydnee admits, "I'm actually not on social media." She smirks. "I know, I know, it's hard to believe. Last year I deleted all my accounts. I just couldn't take it anymore. I was so tired of seeing everyone's posts about how great their life was, when mine was such a train wreck."

"Wow! You deleted *all* your accounts? I don't think I could live without social media. I have hundreds of friends on there. Get this, last week I hit five hundred followers." Trevor pauses. "It's crazy to think that many people are interested in my life." He takes a deep inhale. "You know what, I posted about a new watch I bought yesterday and it got over *55 likes* in less than three hours. I think I'm up to at least 20 comments. It's crazy. I can't even keep up with my replies."

Impressed, Sydnee doesn't hide her admiration. "That's amazing. You must have a great life. I would post about my photography, or volunteering at the animal shelter, and would get nothing—crickets. No one cared. I'd be lucky to get 10 likes. It was depressing, so I just stopped posting. Then I deleted every-single-social-media-app, one-by-one. I have to tell you: I feel so much better now. I stopped comparing my life to other people's. It was invigorating: like a rebirth or a cleanse."

Trevor cringes at that thought. "I give you credit. I couldn't do it. Actually, I think people would miss seeing my posts, to be honest. I can't disappoint my followers. You know what I'm saying?"

"I hear you. Listen, everyone has to do what's best for them. Anyway, you've listened to me ramble on long enough. Let me get the ball rolling here. Give me one second." Sydnee picks up the phone and uses her softest voice over the speaker system: "Donnie to the front desk. Donnie to the front desk. Customer is waiting." She hangs up the receiver and looks at Trevor. "Donnie should be with you shortly. You're welcome to grab a soda, coffee, or bottled water in our customer lounge. We just renovated it. Wait until you see the leather massage chairs. They're incredible. There's also a full-service café for all our customers. When you buy a car from Dean De Carlo's, you're issued a café card that gets you unlimited food and snacks."

Trevor's eyes widen. "That's insane! I don't believe it. I'd probably stop in every day just to put air in my tires."

"If you think that's cool, we also have a mini-gym in the back with a few treadmills and a couple of Peloton bikes. You can work out while your car is being serviced." Sydnee smiles in anticipation of Trevor's reaction.

"That's it! Where's Donnie? I'm buying a car sight unseen. Just give me access to the café and gym." Trevor chuckles at his own humor. "Anyway, it was great meeting you. Take care." He dashes away and then turns around. "Hey, Sydnee. You should reconsider getting back on social media. You're missing out."

Sydnee smiles. "I'm good, but I appreciate it." She waves good-bye.

Trevor enters the service lounge. His jaw drops open and he mumbles, "Oh my God. This place is surreal." He eases himself into the massage chair and gets comfortable. Trevor pulls out his cell phone and snaps a selfie of himself reclined, flashing a peace sign with his fingers. He gets up and walks into the gym.

A man enters the room wearing a pique-knit polo tucked into his dress slacks, and he's holding a clipboard with a stack of forms. He extends his hand. "Trevor?"

"Yeah, that's me." Trevor is sitting on the Peloton bike, pretending he's racing. "This has to be the coolest dealership I have ever seen." He shakes the man's hand.

The man clicks the end of his pen and checks a box on his new client form. "Well, looks like I can sign off that you know all about the café and gym. I'm Donnie. Let's find a car and get a deal done today. How does that sound?"

Trevor snaps a selfie of himself sitting on the Peloton bike. "Sounds great. Let's do it!" Trevor hops off the bike and follows Donnie in the direction of the showroom. "I know *exactly* which car I want."

"Well, the good news is with the Winter Enchantment promotion, every one of my clients has been approved for financing. Welcome to your new home, my friend." Donnie leads Trevor to the showroom to look at floor models.

The Next Day:
Town Walking Track – "The Oval"

"I can't believe it, man! The sales guy told me out of all his customers I'm the only one who didn't get approved for financing. I swear, I have the worst luck." Trevor kicks a pinecone into the street. "I don't know what I'm gonna do. My car is on its last leg, not to mention I look freakin' homeless driving around in that jalopy. Do you know how embarrassing it is to drop the kids off at school in a 15-year-old minivan?"

"It happens…don't sweat it. Try to enjoy this amazing weather. How often is the temperature in the 60s at the end of November?" Paul puts his arm around Trevor's shoulders. "Hey, look on the bright side: at least you have a car."

It's me, Trevor. I'm the guy in this story. And that's my best friend, Paul Mintz. We go for walks whenever we can. I know it sounds like a simple outing, but it's helped me deal with all the stress and turmoil in my life. There is something cathartic about being outside with a friend and discussing daily challenges.

Paul is a psychologist, so I guess you could say, at least recently, these walks have become my unofficial therapy sessions.

"Stop being so positive, Paul. It drives me nuts. Thankfully, I was able to snap a couple of photos of me in the lounge and gym. You wouldn't believe how fancy they were." Trevor pulls out his phone and swipes through those pictures.

Paul slides his sunglasses down the bridge of his nose and squints. "Wow. That's amazing. Is that a Peloton?"

Trevor can't contain himself. "Yes! It was unbelievable. They had treadmills, some dumbbells—and the best part, if you buy a car from this dealership, you get a café card. Unlimited snacks and soda. Check out this photo of the cars." Trevor touches the screen to magnify the image. "That's the model I was going to get. I narrowed the color down to the red or black. I have a picture of me sitting in each car," Trevor says, unable to hide his disappointment.

"Oh, boy. I know that look. Please, don't do it. I'm begging you." Paul slides his sunglasses back up.

Trevor chuckles. "What? These pictures are incredible Facebook material. I can't waste them. I have the entire post mapped out in my mind. It's going to be epic. Hear me out on this one." The men stop walking. Trevor's exaggerated hand gestures add to the suspense. "I'm going to keep the post simple. It's going to be titled, *Saturday Shenanigans.* I'll write: 'Was bored, so I decided to go car shopping. The Black Beauty or the Red Robin?' Then I'll post a picture of me sitting in each car. What do you think? How awesome is that?"

"I think it's ridiculous. What the hell are you going to say when people see you driving the same minivan around town?" Paul shakes his head in disbelief of the juvenile idea.

Trevor is one step ahead. "Dude, I knew you were going to bring that up. I have the perfect alibi. It's simple. Because of the pandemic, my new car is on backorder. The car industry has been slammed by supply-chain delays. I'm not making that up. It's being discussed all over the news."

"What am I gonna do with you, Trev? Just don't post the cheesy picture of you sitting in the massage chair. You look like you're taking a dump. Let's hurry up and finish our walk. I gotta drop the kids off at karate." Paul nudges Trevor to get moving.

Trevor flicks Paul's earlobe. "Fine. I won't post the one of me sitting in the massage chair, but I can't waste the photo of me chillin' on the Peloton. Those bikes are super popular right now. Most people can't afford one. I'll bet that picture is good for at least 60 likes, easy."

Paul shakes his head and responds with his usual subtle sarcasm. "You and your likes. I'm sure Stacey and the kids love hearing you talk about that stuff."

"Aw, they just don't understand the whole concept of social media. Not many people do." Trevor takes out his phone again and catches Paul off guard. "Hey, smile!" Trevor snaps a candid photo of himself and Paul standing next to each other.

> Paul always gives me a hard time about my social media accounts. He thinks I post way too much, but he misses the point of why I do it. It's my opportunity to build my personal brand. I think of every post like a press release. Sure, sometimes, I may *tweak* certain events in my day, but hey, doesn't everyone? In my opinion, there's nothing better than creating content and seeing those likes and comments roll in. It's my chance to escape all the stress and trauma in my life and create my own reality.

A Social Illusion

Chapter Two

Behind the Filter

T revor pulls into his driveway and walks inside his house. "Hey, I'm home! What do you guys want to do today? Is anyone up for taking a ride over to the Camel Back Zoo? It's probably our last chance to see all the animals before they close for the winter."

Trevor's 10-year-old son, Luke, meets his father at the front door. Luke's arms are crossed and his scowl is fierce. "Dad, what's wrong with you? Mom's been in her room crying since you left this morning. I'm so tired of you two fighting every day. You think we wanna go to the stupid zoo with you?"

"Oh stop. She started it. Anyway, it's none of your business. Stay out of it, bud." Trevor peers around for his daughter. "Where's Olivia?"

Luke snaps back at his father. "She's in the back yard on the hammock, reading."

Trevor walks outside and shouts to Olivia, "Yo! What's going on?" He grabs the hammock like a swing, pulls it back, and then let's go.

"Dad, what the heck are you doing? I'm gonna flip over!" Olivia sits up and pushes her father. "What's going on? How was your walk with Paul?"

Trevor sighs, "It was fine. We walked around the Oval in front of the high school. What are you up to?"

Olivia holds up her book. "Reading, duh. Well, I was, until you came out here and disturbed me."

"Jeez, it's like you don't want to spend time with me anymore. Remember the good ol' days when I would give you piggyback rides around the trees? It makes me sad that you're growing up so fast. You're not the little girl with pigtails anymore." Trevor thinks back to those sweet times.

Olivia lies back down. She places her hands behind her head and gets comfortable. "Dad, I'm going to be 14 years old in a few months. I still love you, but I need my space. You know, like most teenagers do. Don't take it personal, OK?"

"I try not to, but I just miss the days when you and your brother were little, that's all. Even though your mom and I spent our weekends chasing you around, life was simpler back then." Trevor sits on the edge of the hammock.

"You gotta stop living in the past and focus on the present, like your marriage. Me and Luke are tired of you both arguing, Dad. And the worst part: it's always about stupid stuff. Like who ate all the cashews or making the drive out to see Grandma. I get married couples have disagreements once in a while, but you guys argue all the time." Olivia tries to nudge her father off the hammock.

Trevor stands up and asks, "When did you become so smart? It must be from all those books you read. I better watch out; you're going to be giving *me* advice soon."

"Get off social media." Olivia's response is blunt.

Trevor steps back and attempts to process his daughter's demand "Why would you say something like that?"

"Because it upsets Mom." Olivia storms inside. Trevor sits down on the edge of the hammock and rocks back and forth.

> My social media hobby is something my wife and I never speak about. I know she isn't a big fan of my posting as often as I do, but I have a lot to share with my friends—all 500 of them. I mean, my life is interesting and people enjoy seeing my content. Sometimes, I think she gets a tad jealous, because I get so much attention from my followers. No matter how many times I try and explain to her how exhilarating social media is, she doesn't want any part of it. It's frustrating, but I can't let her skewed point of view slow down my momentum.

Later That Day:

"Dad, I can't believe you're dragging us to the zoo. We don't want to go. Turn the car around and head home! Mom, please, tell him we hate coming here." Luke whines and grunts.

Stacey rolls her eyes. "Your father seems to think he's the only one in charge. Another day of doing everything he wants. Just make the best of it, Luke. We're almost there. We'll buy you and your sister lunch at the zoo café. I know you like eating there."

"That's the *only* good thing about going to the zoo. I couldn't care less about the stupid giraffes and monkeys." Luke has a moment of clarity. "Oh, can I get one of the giant chocolate chip cookies and a large fruit punch?"

Trevor turns into the lot and parks. "Sure, bud. Hey, who wants to go on the choo-choo train? Whoop whoop!"

"Dad, that train is for kids. Give it up already. We're not going on it. If you want a baby so bad, you and mom should have another one." Olivia chuckles at that thought and looks for agreement from Luke.

Stacey finds the comment absurd. "I wouldn't buy a car with him, let alone have another child. I already have *three* kids." Stacey looks at Olivia, Luke, and Trevor. "I don't want another one. Speaking of cars, Trevor, whatever happened at the dealership? You said you would have *no problem* buying a car with the financing promotion they were running. Stacey's animosity bubbles to the surface. "Ever since you invested our entire savings into that damn gourmet muffin store, our credit score is in the toilet!"

"Uh, the car dealership? Yeah, well, right now I'm just thinking about which color I want to get. The sales guy ran my credit and it was fine. Stop making a big deal about the damn muffin store. It wasn't all our savings." Trevor bites his nails as a sign of guilt.

Stacey crosses her arms and glares at her husband. "Yeah, you're right, it was only 99 percent of our savings. I swear, you can never just admit when you're wrong!"

"Can you both knock it off? My God! Who the heck wants to listen to you two argue nonstop? I don't think either of you understands how awful it sounds: like nails scraping across a chalkboard. Cut-it-out!" Olivia shrieks and slams her head back into the seat.

Trevor glares at Stacey and mumbles, "You started it, as usual."

"Shut up, Trevor! Put that on your social media." Stacey is quick to exit the car. She slams the door closed and speed-walks to the ticket booth.

Luke tries to be the voice of reason. "Dad, listen to me. I know sometimes mom starts the fight, but you have to stop overreacting. When you get upset it makes it worse. Trust me on this one. And you gotta stop posting *everything* on your Facebook and Instagram accounts. Mom hates when you do it."

"I'll try and ignore her, but my posting on social media has nothing to do with anything. Do you even know how many friends I have on Facebook?" Trevor looks into the rearview mirror to see Luke's reaction.

Olivia kicks the back of Trevor's seat. "No one cares, Dad. Get it through your thick skull. And only Boomers use Facebook."

"Jeez. You guys are rough on your old man." Trevor takes a sip of water. "I hate to disappoint you, but I ain't no Boomer. I'm a Gen-Xer. Don't rush my life away."

Luke opens his door. "Let's go. Mom's waiting for us. Also, Dad, *do not* embarrass us today. I'm not wearing those stuffed animal hats in the gift shop like last time. And don't ask me to ride the ponies." Everyone exits the car.

At the *Mammals of the Oceans* exhibit, Stacey and the kids are entertained by the seals propelling themselves throughout the massive tank.

Luke's stomach growls. "Mom, what time is lunch? When can we go eat? I'm freakin' starving."

"Where the heck is your father? He always wanders off." Stacey looks for her husband and spots him sitting at the polar bear photo station. He's scrolling on his phone, oblivious that his family wants to leave. "Luke, go get him, before I lose it. I swear, he only cares about himself."

Luke cups his hands around his mouth and lets out a blood-curdling scream, "Dad, get your butt over here, now!" People walking past them are startled by the commotion, and stare.

Trevor reacts like a jolt of electricity struck him. He drops his phone, picks it up, and dashes over. "What the hell was that, Luke? Everyone in the zoo is looking at us! You're out of control. You lost your iPad and gaming systems when we get home."

Luke throws his arms into the air. "What the hell, Dad?"

Olivia scolds Trevor and joins the rant. "All you do is look at your stupid phone all day! You're the one who dragged us to the zoo."

Stacey storms over and rages, "Your typical bullshit, Trevor! Hope you're happy that you ruined our day and got both kids so upset."

"Are you freakin' kidding me? All I did was check my work e-mail and you all are acting like I committed a crime." Trevor notices a zoo employee wearing a penguin costume. "Guys, look over there." He points at the small crowd of people taking photos with the penguin. "That would be a great family picture. Let's hustle over. I'll buy everyone ice cream if you smile and act like you're actually having a great time." Trevor puts on the full court press. "You can get *two* scoops."

Luke and Olivia smirk as they envision the tasty treat. They reply in unison, "Fine."

Trevor looks at Stacey. "You in?"

"If it will shut you up, sure." Stacey shakes her head in disgust.

Trevor dashes over to secure a spot in line for the photo op. Stacey, Luke, and Olivia trudge behind him. "Guys, hustle up. We're next." Trevor can't contain his excitement. He hands his phone to the zoo employee who's in charge of taking the photographs. The man, in his eighties, has a bushy white mustache and is bald.

Trevor places his arm around the penguin. Stacey and the kids slide into position.

The employee signals he's ready to take the picture by raising his hand. "Waddle, waddle, smile at the camera, gang."

Trevor mumbles instructions to his family: "Look like you're having a good time, please. The biggest smile gets an extra topping on their ice cream."

"OK, I got the money shot! Wow, I'm good," the photographer brags. He looks at Trevor and hands the phone back. "You know something, you're a lucky guy to have such a beautiful family. Everyone looks so happy."

Irritated by that last comment, Stacey and the kids flee the scene. They leave Trevor behind.

The photographer leans in and his chin trembles. His voice is soft and monotone. "Please, son, don't take one minute of life for granted. Before you know it, you'll be standing where I am." The old man limps away and Trevor is dumbfounded by that impromptu plea.

Chapter Three

Surf and Turf

Trevor walks inside the restaurant and sees Paul sitting at the bar. He navigates through the crowd and pulls up the empty bar stool. He grabs a menu and high-fives Paul. "What's going on, man? This place is packed for a Wednesday night. It's weird seeing the moms from drop-off all dolled up." Trevor admires the two brunettes sitting across at the high top.

"Watch it or I'll tell Stacey you're reading the menu…and I'm not talking about the one in your hand. You're lucky as hell, dude. You have one of the most attractive wives in the entire town." Paul takes a sip of his beer.

Trevor sighs. "Thanks, man. Things have been rocky between Stacey and me lately. I feel like all we do is argue. We can't agree on anything."

"Wow. Really? You guys always look happy on your social media posts. I saw the picture you posted the other day at the Camel Back Zoo. If I didn't know any better, I'd swear you had the perfect marriage. You guys are always doing fun things. Hockey games, Broadway shows. That beach house you rented in the summer looked amazing. I remember all the pictures you posted on Instagram. It looked like paradise." Paul is shocked by Trevor's heartfelt admission.

Trevor rolls his neck back and forth and takes a deep breath. "You know, you're the only one I can open up to about these things." Trevor takes a moment to gather his thoughts. "I've been really struggling between the stress at home and work. I can barely sleep at night. I've gained 20 pounds in the last three months. I stopped going to the gym. Work is a mess. I've been doing everything I can to get the promotion, but that guy Doug Fitzberg I told you about is sabotaging me."

"Jeez, man. I'm gonna need a shot of vodka and a cigarette after listening to your episode of Dear Abby." Paul is impressed with his own humor.

Trevor elbows Paul in the shoulder. "Thanks for the heartfelt support. I hope you don't treat your patients as crappy as you do your best friend. I'm pouring my heart out over here. Anyway, I'm starving. I think I'm going to go with the surf and turf tonight." Trevor jokes, "If my credit card is declined, I'll shovel your driveway the next snowstorm to make it up to you."

"Yeah, nice try. The funny thing is, I enjoy shoveling my driveway. Sometimes life moves so fast and furious that doing something as simple as shoveling snow brings me peace. Not to mention, I also feel accomplished, because when I'm done, my driveway is clear. The older we get, the more difficult it is to see progress." Paul snaps his fingers. "Remember when we were kids, our parents would make us clean up our room, organize our bookshelves, and make our bed? Those were things that gave us instant gratification. Try something simple next time when things get chaotic. You'll be surprised how centered you will feel when you're done."

Trevor pretends to fall off his bar stool. "Now that's deep. I'm going to start calling you Yoda. That's great advice, bud. I appreciate it. It makes sense and I will definitely try it. Now let's order some grub before I pass out."

> Paul's perspective on life's challenges blew me away. The way he would weave his advice into the conversation was unique. I felt like he was never judging me or trying to tell me how to live. His insight was subtle, but it made a lasting impression.
>
> I felt like I was spiraling out of control in every direction. Paul was right. No matter how much effort I put into something, I couldn't seem to see any progress. The harder I worked the more blurry and discombobulated things became. Whether it was my marriage, my job, or my children, I believed I was letting everyone down, including myself. Even smiling took effort. Thankfully, I had my safe place, social media. It was the one thing that was always grounded. It was like a blank canvas and I controlled every brush stroke. I was grateful for it.

The Next Day:

Trevor finishes pressure washing the concrete patio slab in his back yard. Stacey walks outside. "Did you fill up my gas tank after your date with Paul last night?"

Trevor smacks his forehead. "Damn, I totally forgot. I'm sorry. I'll do it later today. I promise."

"Please forgive me if I don't believe you. Just like you were going to pick up Olivia on time at gymnastics last week. Your word means nothing to me anymore. It's amazing, you always seem to find time for your friends on social media, but not your family. By the way, why the hell are you buying Surf and Turf at Tuscan's?"

Trevor scratches his head. "How did you know I bought Surf and Turf?"

"I saw your stupid Instagram post about it." Stacey mocks Trevor. "'A little celebration for a great week!' What the hell is that supposed to mean? What the fuck are you celebrating, Trevor? Tell me? Us being broke and not having a penny to our name? The worst part is you try and throw a fishing line into a lake. It's like you purposely *want* people to ask you, what are you celebrating, Trevor? Like something great actually happened. The comments people left made me sick. My God. You were getting congratulations from dozens of people for no reason. Grow up!" Stacey clenches her fists and storms inside.

Trevor kicks his power washer into the grass and his nostrils flare. "Damn it!" He looks up and sees Olivia staring back through an opened window. Trevor walks away and pounds his fist against the house.

Chapter Four

A Promotional Fantasy

New York City: Trevor's Office – 9:00 a.m.

"Hey, Trev. How about those Knicks? They pulled it out at the last minute." Trevor's longtime co-worker, Cliff, sets his backpack on his desk.

Trevor checks the score on his phone. "Dude, you guys beat the freakin' Timberwolves by two points. They're the worst team in the league. How many times do I need to tell you, the Knicks aren't winning anything? They better have their travel agent on speed dial, 'cause they're gonna start summer vacation early."

"Yeah, yeah. Just let me enjoy a win without ripping on me, OK? Anyway, what's going on with the promotion? I heard through the grapevine that you and Fitzberg are the only two who put in for it." Cliff sips his coffee and ponders that thought. "I don't know, Trev, it sounds like *a lot* of work and extra headaches for poquito mas dinero, if you ask me."

Trevor cracks open a frosted can of Mountain Dew and then yanks a McDonald's bag from his backpack. "I hear you, but Stacey is slathering on the guilt about my investing in that muffin store. Every day she's pressuring me to make more money. Listen, even if it's just a couple hundred bucks a month, it's worth not hearing her bitch and complain. Plus, who doesn't love a promotion?" Trevor makes sure the coast is clear. "Between us, Fitzberg doesn't have a shot at getting this promotion over me. I got it locked up, my man." Trevor takes a bite of his sausage biscuit and winks.

Later That Day – Trevor's Supervisor's Office

Trevor grits his teeth. "Come on, Keith, you gotta be kidding me! I nailed the Belmont Project, and crushed the Amelia presentation. Hell, their vice president even sent you an email that said I was the reason they signed the contract. This doesn't make any sense. How does Fitzberg beat me out?" Trevor stops pacing but is reluctant to sit down.

Keith raises his eyebrow. "How did you know about the Amelia email?"

"You forwarded it to me." Trevor rolls his eyes and gets serious. "Listen, Keith, we both know I've worked my ass off the last year. I've done everything you've asked me to do and more. I'm one of the first people in the office and the last one out the door. I just don't believe this. I really don't."

Keith closes the door. "Can you calm down and let me explain why we made the decision we did? This wasn't something we took lightly. John and I went back and forth on this for days."

"Trevor looks up at the ceiling and taps his foot. "Yeah. I'm all ears, Keith. Please, enlighten me, because I'm mentally sitting in a dark cave right now. I feel like I'm suffocating."

Keith sits down and closes his laptop. He puts his cell phone on silent mode. "I'm just gonna be 100 percent transparent with you. I'm a straight shooter and always have been." Keith doesn't hold back. "The last couple of months you've lost your focus. Shit, Trevor, everyone was talking about how you dozed off during the department meeting with John last week. If Jeremy didn't elbow you, your puddle of drool would have dripped all over the table. Donna has come to me *four times* in the last month alone, because you keep making errors in every damn proposal. I'm pissed, because you're better than this. If Donna hadn't caught those mistakes, Trevor, they would have cost us hundreds of thousands of dollars. You were always my lieutenant, second in charge, but something's going on. Maybe I should have had this conversation with you sooner, but I kept hoping things would snap back into place for you. I'm not even going to discuss how many times I see you scrolling on your cell phone all day. It's like you're glued to that fuckin' thing. Talk to me, Trevor: what's going on with you?"

Keith's observations are spot on. Trevor walks to the mini fridge. He grabs a can of Coke, chugs it, and belches. "I don't know what's going on with me, Keith. That's the honest answer. Something's not right. I haven't been able to sleep, my anxiety has been off the charts, and I feel like I'm losing interest in the things I used to enjoy doing." Trevor sits down and sweat percolates on his forehead. "This isn't easy for me to talk about. I keep praying I'm gonna wake up one morning and everything will bounce back into place."

"First and foremost, I'm here for you. That hasn't changed. Work is important, but your mental health needs to be the priority right now. Do you want to take some time off? You should have a ton of vacation saved up. I don't think you've taken any in a while. Whatever you need, just let me know." Keith's empathy is soothing.

Trevor leans back in his chair and studies Keith's expression. "I appreciate it, but I'm fine. I'll fight through this and figure things out. I'm just going through a few bumps right now. I'll push harder at work and make sure I pick up the pace."

"Well, please consider taking some time off. Just a heads up: our insurance plan covers six free sessions with a licensed mental health therapist. Sometimes talking about things can make a big difference." Keith glances at a picture of his children.

Trevor is quick to reply, "I'm good. Trust me. I probably shouldn't have said anything. You won't have to have this conversation with me again. I promise." Trevor walks over to the door and looks back. "Oh, and I'm sorry about being on the phone so much. Lately, checking my social media posts is the only thing that seems to bring me a little joy."

"I wouldn't know. I've never had an interest in that stuff. Before you leave, I do have a little bit of positive news," Keith is eager to share.

Trevor's eyes widen and he stands at attention. "Positive news? God knows I could use some of that now. Are we getting a chunky Christmas bonus?"

"Yeah, I wish that were the case. John told me this morning that our department is realigning job titles. Each person has a different one depending on the year they started. HR said it's a mess and there needs to be consistency. Starting Monday, regardless of current position, everyone on my team will have a title change to Associate Marketing Manager."

"Wow! That's incredible, Keith. You're right, that is some positive news." Trevor bounces on his toes.

Keith clarifies, "It's *only* your job title, not your paycheck. I just wanna make sure you don't get too excited.

"I'll take what I can get." Trevor grins and walks out.

At the Oval:

The brisk fall breeze shoots the falling leaves through the air. Trevor and Paul pick up the pace as they scurry back to their cars.

Trevor rubs his hands together. "Damn, it's getting cold. I should have worn my winter coat. It sucks: in another couple of weeks all the trees are gonna look dead." Trevor wipes his drippy nose. "It's 4:30 in the afternoon and it looks like it's nighttime. It's so depressing. Have I ever told you I hate winter?"

"Every time I see you," Paul jokes. "Try and find the positives. I hate to be so harsh, but it's not just about you. Sometimes your happiness needs to derive from the joy of others. You've told me your kids love growing up here. I see all the pictures you post of them: diving into leaf piles, sledding at the elementary school, pummeling each other with snowballs. Man, when you're a kid, these are the best months of the year." Paul pauses and elbows Trevor. "Hey, you smell that?"

Trevor lifts up his head and crinkles his nose. His sniffing noises amuse Paul. "I don't smell anything. What am I missing?"

"You don't smell that nostalgic wood-burning aroma? Look over there." Paul points at the smoke bellowing from chimneys.

Trevor chuckles, "Well, yeah, I smell that. I thought you meant something else. Dude, what's your point here? I'm lost."

"My point is that you can always find something positive buried within every situation. Sometimes, it's the things right in front of us.

Like the smell of wood burning on a cold, invigorating, fall after-noon. We choose how we want to see the world." Paul puts his arm around Trevor's shoulders. "Oh, I completely forgot. Congrats on the big promotion at work. I saw you posted your new *fancy* job title on Facebook: Associate Marketing Manager. I dig the message you wrote: *Hard work pays off.* It's so simple, but true. Hopefully, they threw you a little extra bread, if you know what I'm saying."

Trevor bites his nails. "Oh, yeah, the promotion. Thanks, I appre-ciate it. My boss took care of me. Let's just say, I'll be getting that new car sooner than later."

For the first time, I found myself 'bending the truth' to Paul about one of my social media posts. I was mentally drained—and to be honest, I just didn't feel like getting into the details. Not to mention, within one day, I had over 25 comments and 85 likes on that post. Do you know how good it felt to read all those congratulatory remarks? I was sink-ing faster than a concrete block and that positive reinforcement was the boost I desperately need-ed. I mean, "technically" it was a promotion, right? Luckily, I pay the bills and manage our checking account, so I'm hoping Stacey doesn't notice the small raise that I never got. Anyway, Olivia's sleep-away camp tuition was due and I needed to figure out how I was going to come up with the deposit. It was going to take some schmoozing, but there was one person I could always count on: someone who never let me down.

Chapter Five

Family Heirlooms

T revor treks up the rugged terrain. The morning dew covers the ground and a blanket of leaves lines the dirt road. The pastel-colored sunrise breaks through the sky. Trevor's footsteps startle the squirrels as they scurry up the massive oak trees. The stream trickles along the sides of the path. Trevor approaches a 1940s Cape-Cod–style house with a gravel driveway. A 1976 AMC Pacer, riddled with rust, is parked inside the carport. Filled with anticipation, Trevor knocks on the screen door and steps back.

The door cracks open and Trevor sees a watery, red-rimmed eye staring back at him.

"Who's there? I don't have my glasses on," a tender, fragile voice questions.

Trevor projects his voice and beams, "It's me, Grandma. You know, your favorite and best-looking grandson. Sorry I didn't call you first. I was passing through town and thought I would stop in and say hi."

The door chain lock rattles and slides open. Grandma wastes no time with her witty response: "Well, lucky for you I can't see well anymore, so I wouldn't know if you're good looking or not. Come inside, honey. It's cold out." Grandma peers through the window blinds. "Where's your car?"

Trevor hugs his grandmother and hangs his jacket on the coat rack. The wood burning inside the fireplace pops and crackles. "I parked by the mailbox. It's the perfect morning for a walk. I needed to clear my head and take a little break."

Grandma pats the seat cushion. "Come, sit down. I just brewed a fresh pot of coffee. Let me grab you a cup." Trevor gets cozy on the tweed couch and unwinds.

"Here you go, my sweet boy. Drink this, it will warm you up." Grandma's withered hands tremor as she sets the mug on the coffee table.

"Thank you, Grandma." Trevor sips the steaming beverage. "You always take good care of me. How have you been feeling?"

"I'm doing OK. My arthritis slows me down, but please, don't worry about me. So, tell me, your mother mentioned you received a big promotion at work. That's so exciting. I guess she only found out because you shared it on the Internet. I'll tell you: I don't know how you kids constantly put your life story out there so the world can read about it. You know, not everything has to be shared."

Trevor chuckles and explains, "Grandma, the Internet is the platform to be able to go on all the different apps. What you're referring to is called social media. Everyone has an account." Trevor sits up and gets excited. "Are you kidding me? It's the greatest thing in the world! You're able to post pictures and videos of the most exciting events in your life. Imagine, all your friends can like and comment on your content. It's really incredible."

"I don't need to imagine and not everyone has an account, 'cause I don't and even if I were your age, I wouldn't." Grandma doesn't hide her disgust. "Apps, rapps, whatever they're called, it's not necessary. My God, sharing every little detail that goes on. When I was your age, we celebrated our successes and milestones with our family members: the ones who really cared. That was enough for us."

Trevor is caught off guard by the unexpected rant and explains the rules: "You're not allowed to talk to Mom before I come over anymore. Jeez, she got you all fired up, Grandma. There's a reason I don't tell Mom much about my life: she's always judging everyone. I'd rather she find out on social media than from me telling her. Let's change the subject; I've already been down in the dumps and talking about her makes it worse."

"I'm sorry, sweetheart. I didn't mean to upset you. I agree, let's talk about something else, like my beautiful great-grandchildren. How are they doing?" Grandma looks at Luke and Olivia's framed school photos.

Trevor gears up to discuss Olivia's camp tuition. "Thankfully, the kids are doing great. They enjoy all their after-school activities. Luke is still loving karate and starts indoor soccer this month. Olivia is becoming quite the gymnast and made the honor roll again. Of course, she takes after her dad when it comes to her academics." Trevor thinks back to his school struggles and smirks.

Grandma applauds and beams with pride. "They are really something else. Those kids make me so happy. That reminds me, I have something for them. I'll be right back." Grandma hobbles into her bedroom and Trevor catches up on his social media. He sits back, sips his coffee, and checks his Facebook notifications. He's eager to read the comments on his latest post.

"Oh, will you put that phone away?" Grandma reprimands. She shuffles over and holds a tattered large manila envelope. The metal clasp secures its contents.

Startled, Trevor slides his phone into his pocket. "Uh, sorry, Grandma. Stacey was texting me. She wanted to know when I'd be home. I'm going to pick up bagels for lunch."

"How is my beautiful granddaughter-in-law doing? She's such a good Mommy." Grandma sits next to Trevor and pats his thigh.

Preoccupied with what's inside the envelope, Trevor answers, "Stacey is doing fantastic. Whatcha got there?" Trevor reaches for the envelope and Grandma playfully slaps the top of his hand.

"Well, your children are getting older. Now is the perfect time for me to give them this gift. I've been looking forward to this day for many years. Today just felt like the right time." Grandma presses the envelope to her heart as a gesture that what's inside has senti-mental meaning. She opens the envelope and angles it upside down.

Trevor's heart races as two rings slide out. "Whoa, Grandma, those are beautiful."

"Thank you, sweetie. These are treasures." Grandma picks up the solitaire diamond ring and stares into the stone. Memories from years past surge through her mind. "This was my engagement ring your grandfather gave me. We were planning a quaint, low-key, wedding. We wanted our parents and close family members there—that's it. Neither of us cared about having a big bonanza of a cele-bration. As long as we had the people who loved us there, it was all we needed. In fact, my mother was so upset we wouldn't take the money she offered us. She wanted us to get married at her private country club in Hewlett. It would have cost a fortune. One thing about your grandfather: he never took handouts. He would rather go without, before taking a penny from someone. I often wonder what our wedding would have been like had he made it home from the war." Grandma presses her fist to her lips.

Trevor clears his throat. "That's one of the most stunning rings I've ever seen." Rays of light sparkle atop the polished stone.

"Thank you, dear. Your grandfather had an uncle in the diamond business. His name was Eli and he hired your grandfather for one summer. Instead of paying your grandfather money, Eli gave him this." Grandma hands the treasured ring to Trevor and she smiles.

Trevor's hand shakes as the keepsake rests in his palm. "It's like I'm holding a piece of your life in my hand."

"You are." Grandma places her palm under Trevor's hand. Her fingers guide his fist closed. "It's Olivia's ring now. One day I hope the beauty of this diamond reminds her of how much she is loved. May my princess always shine bright like this precious stone."

Tears well in Trevor's eyes. "Come on, Grandma. You're making me emotional over here."

Grandma picks up the other ring, a solid gold wedding band. "I never had a chance to put this on your grandfather's finger. I pray one day Luke's wife will place it on his ring finger."

"Wow. I don't know what to say, Grandma." Trevor places his hand on his chest and catches his breath. He admires a photo of his youthful grandparents displayed on the mantle.

Grandma smiles and tears trickle down her face. She places the wedding band into Trevor's hand. Both rings lay side-by-side. "There's nothing to say."

Trevor rests his head on his grandmother's shoulder. "I love you, Grandma."

Chapter Six

Blind Envy

Thunder rattles the car windows and raindrops pelt the hood. Trevor grabs his umbrella from underneath the seat and makes a run for it. He weaves around the lake-size puddles in the parking lot. The swooping wind gust flips Trevor's umbrella inside out. He stomps his foot and shouts, "I can't catch a break!" He chucks the ruined umbrella into the bushes. Lightning bolts shoot down from the sky. Trevor finds shelter underneath the awning of the gymnastics studio and uses the bottom of his shirt to wipe his face.

"Hey! You looked like you just swam in a lake. What's going on?" A striking petite brunette with green eyes tosses Trevor a hand towel.

Trevor dries his hair. "You're a life saver, Beth. Why the heck did you have a towel on you?"

"I always pack a couple in Sammy's gymnastics bag. You gotta be prepared." Beth winks and smiles. "What have you been up to? It's been so long since I've seen you."

Trevor is eager to catch up. "I've been awesome. I can't complain. Just super busy, you know: work, the kids, never a minute to rest."

"Oh my Gosh, congratulations on the promotion at work. I saw your post on Facebook, *Mister-big-man-on-campus.*" Beth gets playful and touches Trevor's shoulder. "Oh, and I also saw on Instagram you signed up Olivia for sleep-away camp. I am so jealous. I wish I could send Sammy to Timber Pines, too. I looked at the tuition for the first half of the summer and nearly fell out of my chair. Your daughter is *so* lucky: whitewater rafting, jet skis, and hiking. Does life get any better?"

Trevor scratches the back of neck and grins. "Thanks! Olivia is pretty excited. I'm grateful I've made some lucky investment decisions over the years."

"Well, I wish my life was more like yours. You have the *perfect* family. Everyone looks so happy and content in the photos you post: Not that I stalk you on social media or anything." Beth sighs. "You know, I can barely get through a day. Between my divorce, Sammy's OCD, and taking care of my mother, some mornings I don't want to get out of bed. Anyway, I have to run and pick up dinner for Sammy while she's in gymnastics class. She loves to eat in the car on the way home. It's definitely not as exciting as sleep-away camp, but it makes me feel like I'm a good mommy—well, at least for a little bit, anyway." Beth waves goodbye and dashes away.

Trevor looks at his watch and mumbles. "Oh, crap!" Still dripping with water, he rushes inside.

Olivia stands in front of the doorway with her hands on her hips. "What the hell, Dad? You *promised* me you'd be here to watch my routine." Olivia's elbow to Trevor's stomach was intentional. "Mom's right. You only care about yourself. Let's go." Olivia rushes outside as Trevor stands motionless. He watches a father cheer for his toddler-aged daughter. Trevor takes a purposeful breath and mopes to the car.

Chapter Seven

Paid in Full

Sunday Morning: Brookside Diner

Paul's chuckle camouflages his unease. He shakes his head and exclaims, "No way—I don't believe it! Even you wouldn't sink that low."

Trevor's silence is an admission of guilt.

"Please tell me you didn't do that, Trevor. I'm starting to think you're not joking." Paul crosses his fingers.

Trevor looks down, rests his head on his fingertips and massages his own forehead. "I'm going to hell, aren't I?"

"You sold your grandmother's engagement ring that was a gift for your daughter? Yeah, man. I'd say hell would be a step up from where you should be right now." Paul looks serious.

Trevor pushes his plate away. "I've lost my appetite. I really screwed up. If Stacey finds out, I'm gonna be living in the shed. I swear, every decision I make seems to be the wrong one."

"The fact that you are using the money to send Olivia to camp is understandable, to a degree. You're trying to do something special for your daughter. No one can fault you for that. The part I question is how much of that decision was for your social media reel?" Paul cuts to the chase. "Listen, I saw the post you made on Instagram."

Paul grabs a pen from the empty table next to him. He writes on his napkin and points at each word as he reads aloud, "'Tuition is paid in full. Timber Pines, here we come!' I mean, are you kidding me? Listen, you're like a brother to me, so I always shoot straight with you. I think I just answered my own question. What did Stacey say when she read your post?"

Trevor slumps in his seat. "I don't think she has seen that camp post yet. We really don't talk much lately unless it's something important about Olivia or Luke. Stacey knows my grandmother helps us out with expenses for the kids, like camp, and extracurricular activities. My grandmother's favorite line is: 'It's their birthday present.' I think the kids have gotten 10 'birthday presents' so far this year. Stacey probably assumes my grandma wrote me another check. I never even told her about the rings. I know my wife: she would go crazy."

"Well, shoot, can you blame her? What about your grandfather's wedding band? Did you sell that, too, so you could buy a new set of golfclubs?" Paul tries to lighten the mood and pretends to putt.

Trevor is quick to set the record straight. "I couldn't sell that for any amount of money. My grandparents picked out that wedding band before my grandfather went off to the war. She never had the chance to put it on his finger. That one is in my safe at home."

"So, you do have a heart. Thank God. I was gonna have to unfriend you if you sold your grandfather's ring. Get it, *unfriend*? Paul is proud of his own humor. "Nothing like a lame social media joke."

Trevor finds the jab in poor taste. "I feel bad enough; I don't need you making it worse." Trevor tosses a handful of sugar packets at Paul. "I feel like someone pulled a lever inside my brain and it's off the tracks. Out of nowhere, I've been having panic attacks at work about the most basic tasks. For example, now I need to take the stairs instead of the elevator. I freak out that I'll get trapped inside." Trevor's face becomes flushed by that thought. "Imagine walking up 24 flights of stairs every day you go to the office. I have to bring an extra undershirt, because I'm drenched in sweat by the time I get to my desk. I make up an excuse when the guys ask me to go down to the café for lunch. Things are tough right now, that's all. I'm trying to hold everything together the best I can. It feels like I'm rollerskating on an ice rink. I can't catch my balance."

"I'm sorry. You know the last thing I would want to do is make you feel worse. The important thing for you to understand is that how you are feeling is normal. I know that sounds odd, but it's the truth. Most people don't feel comfortable speaking about their mental health the same way they do about their physical health. So, when someone is going through life challenges and trauma, they can feel like they're alone on a deserted island." Paul butters his bagel.

Trevor points at Paul. "That's exactly how I've been feeling. I look around and everyone seems happy except me. I think the anxiety and panic attacks are what's causing my depression. Who the hell can live like that every day? I can't even figure out what triggered this."

"Don't spend all your time trying to figure that part out. Sometimes it's an accumulation of traumatic events that you don't realize have piled up. It's like plaque on a tooth. It doesn't get that way overnight. Unfortunately, most people don't make their mental health a priority until it's too late. The good news: there are definitely things you can do to help yourself now." Paul's positivity is comforting.

Trevor breathes lighter. "Well, that makes me feel better. I think my insurance pays for a few therapy sessions, so at least it won't cost me anything. I may call the number on the back of my insurance card and see if the provider can give me the names of a few therapists nearby."

"That's a call I would make sooner than later. It's also important you're aware that other modalities exist besides talk therapy, and of course, the biggest money-maker in the world, big pharma. Our Western psychiatry culture tends to feed people the misconception that those are your only two options, which is not the truth." Paul takes a bite from his bagel and sits back.

Trevor tilts his head. "That's interesting, but what the heck are modalities?"

"OK, here's the best way for me to explain the answer. Stick with me on this one. When you go to your gym, how many exercise machines are there?" Paul gets crafty with his response.

Trevor is unsure how that relates to his question, but he plays along. "I don't know, maybe 50 or so. There are also treadmills, ellipticals, and stationary bikes. I never counted, but there are a lot of options. The bicep station alone has at least 10 different machines you can use." Trevor flexes his arms and stares at his muscles.

"Well, you should start using those machines, with marshmallow arms like those." Paul laughs at his own smack-down. "Anyway, you just answered your own question. If you want to get in better physical condition, you have many different options. Just because bicep curls work great for me, it doesn't mean they will for you. You might choose a different exercise that gives you better results. I know you prefer the step machine, but my knees can't handle it. I'd rather use the stationary bike. The point is, there are a variety of different ways to get into better physical shape. The same applies to our mental health. The frustrating thing for an integrative psychologist like me is the average person doesn't realize it. Like I said, our culture has led everyone to believe there are two ways to treat mental health challenges and it's simply not true."

Trevor's eyes widen and he's quick to type notes into his phone. "This is good stuff, man. So, a modality is another treatment method to improve your health?"

Paul snaps his finger and points at Trevor. "Bingo. That's exactly what it is. And when people feel comfortable talking about their mental health like we are now, it normalizes the conversation. Imagine this: A co-worker asks how you're doing and you answer honestly. You say to that person you're having panic attacks about using the elevator. First off, you'll probably feel better, because you lifted a weight off your shoulders by talking about that fear. Second, you give that person the opportunity to share their life challenges with you. There's a good chance they may have gone through something similar and can share what helped them. You're opening up the communication channel. Now imagine if everyone took this same approach. The flood gates would open up and we would find out *everyone* is on a mental health scale. We may fluctuate throughout our lifetime, but we're all on it. When we recognize the traumas we face impact our central nervous system structures in a similar way, then the 1-in-5 mental health disorder statistic we often hear about becomes a 5-in-5 reality. We *all* have times in our life when we struggle with our mental health. Anyone who tells you different isn't being truthful."

Trevor falls back into his chair and does his best Marty McFly impression: "Whoa, that was heavy, Doc. I didn't realize I was going to be getting schooled today, but I'm glad I am. I never looked at my mental health that way. I'm already more relaxed, knowing the way I'm feeling is normal. I'm not sure if I ever told you this, but my mother worried about everything. Her thoughts would immediately go to the worst possible scenario. Sometimes, those thoughts were downright terrifying. The worst part is she would voice them out loud. You know, that wears on a child after a while. Before I knew it, I was processing events in my life the same way. For example, when my heartbeat races because of my anxiety, I convince myself I'm having a heart attack. Then it feels like I lose control and my irrational thoughts spiderweb into a million directions. Before I know it, I'm knee-deep in a panic attack. It's a vicious cycle, man."

"I give you a lot of credit for recognizing that pattern. You should be proud of yourself." Paul leans in toward Trevor. "I want to make one thing clear. This is important, so listen up. It's normal to have mental health struggles, but it's imperative you don't stay in that space. Like I said before, mental health is not a one-size-fits-all approach. What works for me might not work for you." Trevor nods and Paul makes his point even more clear: "Listen, I don't mind filling in the gaps, but I want you to see your own therapist. I'd tell my own mother the same thing. I know too much about your life. You need a fresh perspective from a psychologist who doesn't know you. Please, make that call."

Trevor agrees. "It makes sense. I appreciate the honesty. I guess it would be like my mother editing my manuscript. She would tell me every part of the story was great."

"Exactly. Can I mention something I think would help you feel better right off the bat?" Paul is cautious, but proceeds.

Trevor braces for impact. "Go for it. Lay it on me."

"Please consider taking a break from social media." Paul puts his hands together as if he is praying. "I think it would be good for you. You put so much pressure on yourself to post content you think people will react to. It's gotta be draining." Paul leans in again. "I haven't said anything, but I can feel your frustration when you don't get action on your posts."

Trevor crosses his arms and scoots back in his seat. "Real nice, Paul. I'm basically pouring my heart out here and you throw that insult at me? Come on, man. That's just wrong." Trevor struggles to stay calm. "First of all, I don't post anything to get a reaction. That's the stupidest thing you've ever said. I enjoy sharing happy occasions that happen in my life. Do you think I give a crap if someone likes or comments on my posts?"

"Are you *really* sure you want me to answer that?" Paul's sarcasm isn't appreciated.

Trevor stands up and chugs his soda. He glares at Paul. Without warning, Trevor slams his own chair into the side of the table and storms outside.

Paul stares at the writing on the napkin and crumples it up. He pays the tab and leaves.

Chapter Eight

Brotherly Love

Trevor knocks on the front door and paces. After several minutes without a response, he peers through the opened blinds and knocks on the front window.

"Boo!" A male voice startles Trevor from behind him.

Trevor turns around and places his hand over his own heart. "Jeez, dude! You scared the crap out of me. Take it easy on your older brother, will ya? Those extra six years make a big difference." Trevor catches his breath. "So, what's going on? What did you want to give me?"

"Sorry, big bro. I forgot you're only a few years away from becoming a half-century. I have something I think you will love. Let's just say I treated myself, which will in turn benefit you. Come on in." Trevor's brother, Jordan, opens the front door and the men walk inside the house. Trevor takes a step back. "Whoa! That's incredible! I feel like I'm at SeaWorld." Trevor's eyes widen and he wants to take a closer look. "Do you mind?" Trevor asks his brother for approval.

"Go for it. Just don't get too close. Any sudden movement can startle them. Sometimes it causes those little guys to dart into the glass. I don't need any casualties today." Jordan chuckles and turns the aquarium's light on. Live plants sway and the industrial-size filters shoot bubbles throughout the colossal aquatic masterpiece. An array of brightly colored fish weave through the elaborate pirate ship décor.

"Whatcha think?" Jordan grins. "That baby right there is a three-hundred-gallon tank. You aren't gonna find many residential aquariums that big."

Trevor moves to the side of the tank and stares at the fish. "Man, this is incredible. You must have 15 different species of fish in there."

"Actually, 22, but who's counting. Check this feature out." Jordan scrolls through his mobile phone and selects a loop of tranquil instrumental music. The sound projects from a small speaker attached to the base of the fish tank. "I had the tank custom built and that speaker is Bluetooth. There's a fish tank app on my phone that plays relaxing therapeutic music. I can pick from a playlist of thousands of variations."

Trevor is impressed. "Did you get the Rolls Royce of fish tanks? The next thing you're going to tell me is the fish tank light pulses to the rhythm of the music."

Jordan smirks and showboats, "Not only that, but I can change the color of the light." Jordan slides his finger back and forth on his phone screen. "Everything is controlled through the Aquarium App. It's so relaxing to lie on the couch and watch the fish swim with the light and music on. Every night after work it's the first thing I do when I get home. It clears my mind and puts me at ease."

"I may need to start coming over more often and follow your lead." Trevor sighs and leaves Jordan curious by that comment.

"You're always welcome to come over. Is everything OK? I didn't want to say anything, but you look a little stressed out. It's unusual for you not to shave or cut your hair. Not to mention, I can't believe how much gray you have mixed into that beard." Jordan squeezes his brother's shoulders to try and lighten the mood.

Trevor cracks his knuckles and looks at the ceiling. "I don't know what's going on, Jordan. I think maybe it's a combination of different things. It's hard to say for sure." Trevor decides to share some private details. "Please keep this between us, but things have been *very* rocky with Stacey. We can't go more than a few hours without screaming at each other. I'm lucky if the kids say two words to me. I've made a couple of big screwups at work that my boss wasn't happy about. I just can't seem to get my momentum going. It's like I'm in this funk. The more I worry about getting out of it, the more intense my anxiety gets. I feel like I'm running on a hamster wheel."

Jordan is encouraging with his response. "Wow. I'm sorry to hear that. You've always been a warrior and fought through adversity. I'm sure this will pass. I have to admit, though, you caught me off guard a little bit. Mom is always telling me how great you've been doing. I'm confused."

"What do you mean? I barely speak to her. She wouldn't know anything that's going on in my life." Trevor ponders how that could be.

Jordan is swift with his reply. "Mom sees your posts online. Nothing is adding up right now. She told me about your promotion at work, but you're telling me that your boss is upset because you've made mistakes. Last time Mom was here, she showed me pictures of you, Stacey, and the kids. Everyone looked so happy. It's odd, that's all."

"It's complicated, Jordan. That's all I can say. I guess things aren't always as they seem." Trevor rubs his eyes and yawns. "Right now, social media is my outlet while things are so bumpy."

Jordan sprinkles fish food into the tank. Well, deleting all my social media accounts was the best decision I ever made. I was tired of seeing all the 'look how great my life is' posts. Jordan stares into the tank. "I fell for it and compared my life to what I saw on social media. Isn't that sad? Then one day it hit me: in most cases people were posting their highlight reel."

"Highlight reel? What do you mean?" Trevor is floored by his brother's vulnerable confession.

Jordan explains, "You're into sports. Think about when an athlete gets drafted to play professional football, for example. What does the sports network show once the player is selected by an NFL team?"

"The best plays from their college football games: Interceptions, touchdowns, sacks. Everything that makes them look like a great prospect." Trevor's passion for sports is evident.

Jordan gives a thumbs up. "Perfectly stated. The sports network doesn't show the player's dropped passes, failed field goal attempts, or misreads. They show the 20 seconds of brilliance, execution, and success. Imagine a highlight reel full of all the plays that athlete never made. That doesn't make for good television ratings, even though it's the truth. All I'm saying is just be careful, bud. It's easy to get caught up in the alternate realities of what people post. Most are sharing their highlight reel. It just happens to be moments of everyday life events vs. the football field. I hope that makes sense."

Trevor is stunned by his brother's insights. "Yeah, it sure does. The way you explained it is interesting. I've never thought of social media that way."

"Well, now you see why I had to disengage from it. Too much of anything can become toxic." Jordan walks over to the corner of the room. "So, come over here. I have something I want to give you. Hopefully, it will help distract you from all the stress you're dealing with right now." Jordan yanks the bedsheet off of what looks like a large piece of furniture."

Trevor places both of his hands on his head and steps back. "Are you kidding? You're giving that to me? It's incredible."

Jordan puts his arm around Trevor's shoulders. "That's yours now, bud. I won't be needing it anymore since I have my new set-up. Please, enjoy. It's a 150-gallon tank. The filtration system is the best you can buy. I also have a milk crate filled with tank decorations and a fresh bag of gravel. I'll even give you a couple of my Plecos and Cory Catfish."

"I don't know what to say. You could have easily sold the tank and kept the money." Trevor is touched by his brother's generosity. "It's the nicest thing anyone has done for me in a while. It means a lot. This whole visit meant a lot. I needed it. Thanks, little bro. Even though you're not that little anymore. Trevor pats Jordan's plump belly."

Jordan is fast to respond. "I may not be little anymore, but that hairline looks like it's running away from the front of your scalp." The men chuckle and embrace.

Chapter Nine

"Put Down Your Phone!"

Gameplex Video Arcade

"Dad, I think I'm gonna play the claw machine one more time. I'm feeling lucky." Luke kisses his gamecard.

Trevor checks the time on his phone. "Well, you've already blown 40 dollars today on that stupid machine. What's one more time? Go ahead, but we're leaving as soon as you're done. I need to get home. Oh, and by the way, those machines are rigged. No one *ever* wins anything. You're wasting your time."

"Gee, thanks, Dad. Now I'm *actually* depressed." Luke didn't hide his irritation. "Can you at least watch me, please?"

Trevor doesn't look up and thumbs through his phone. "Yeah, yeah, I'll watch you. Go ahead. I'll be right there."

Luke skips over to the claw machine and stands in line. Trevor checks his social media accounts for the latest gossip. He comments on several posts and then checks in, so his followers know he's at Gameplex.

"Yes! I did it! I won! I don't believe it." Luke is beaming as he looks around for his father. He reaches into the drop box to grab his sought-after prize and scans the arcade. "You gotta be kidding me," Luke mumbles. He spots his father, staring at his phone, in deep thought. Luke stomps over and chucks the stuffed animal at Trevor's head. "What are you doing, Dad? I told you to watch me!"

Oblivious, Trevor attempts to conjure up an excuse. "Hey. What was that for? I was answering work emails. Calm down, bud."

"You're a liar, Dad! I know you were on your phone checking stupid Facebook. I can't believe this." Luke kicks the arcade game next to him. "After all these years, I finally won a prize and you were nowhere to be found. Sometimes, I just want to punch you."

Trevor grabs Luke's shoulder. "Hey! You need to calm down. People are staring at us. I told you I was working. Don't be rude, especially in public. You'll be punished. I'm not kidding. When I looked up, I saw you standing in line and the next thing I know you're hitting me with a stuffed animal."

Luke pulls away from his father and struggles to hold back his tears. "Stop making excuses, Dad. It's making it worse. I can never count on you for anything. Mom's right: you're useless."

"Listen, I'm sorry. How can I make it up to you? What if we stop for ice cream on the way home?" Trevor pulls out his standard get-out-of-jail card. He makes the offer more enticing, "I'll let you get an extra topping."

Luke glares at his father and pouts. "I already had ice cream to-day. Mom won't let me have it again."

"I won't tell if you don't tell. Come on, pal. I'll even let you get the fresh-baked waffle cone." Trevor sweetens the bribe. "And, you can have one more ride on the bumper cars."

Luke plays along. "Fine, but I get to drive."

"Consider it done. Just don't slam into the wall. My neck is still sore from the last time you drove." Trevor gives Luke a noogie.

"Grab your stuffed animal. Let's take a picture with you holding your grand prize. You should be proud of yourself. I've never seen anyone win at the claw machine."

Luke's head hangs low. "Now you want to take a picture? Before you didn't care enough to watch me. Dad, I have a question for you: Have you ever thought about how it makes me feel when you ignore me, because of that thing?" Luke points to Trevor's phone. "I want to smash it so bad. I really do."

"I didn't ignore you, pal. I happened to be looking down at my phone the exact second you won your prize. Before that, I was watching the entire time. Trust me. Now let's take that picture in front of the claw machine." Trevor nudges Luke. They walk over and get in position for the selfie. "Big smiles, Lukester. Hold up your stuffed animal like you just won the Stanley Cup."

Luke rolls his eyes and sulks. Reluctant, he raises his prize into the air with two hands. "Just take the stupid picture already, will you?"

"I need smiles not frowns." Trevor tickles Luke and snaps the photo. Then he inspects the candid shot. "Great picture! I'll send it to Mommy."

Luke grabs his father's t-shirt and pulls Trevor in close. "Dad, I'm telling you now, do-not-put-that-picture-on-Facebook. You got it?"

"Ok, ok. I got it." Trevor backs away.

Chapter Ten

A Blast From the Past

Landmark Billiards and Cigar Bar

T revor lines up his pool stick with the center of the cue ball and calls his shot: "Left corner pocket." The 8-ball zips across the pool table like a laser beam and bangs into the pocket of choice. Trevor shimmies and hoists his pool stick in the air. "Who's the man?"

"Not you." Paul laughs and points to the cue ball as it rolls and drops into the pocket.

Trevor shakes his head, not surprised by the stroke of bad luck. "That scratch right there, it's the story of my life. I couldn't think of a better comparison."

"Oh, come on, don't overreact. You have a lot of positives in your life. Try and focus on those. I saw the picture you posted the other day, the one of you and Luke at Gameplex. The little guy looked so happy to be with his pops. I'm sure celebrating his claw machine victory is a memory he'll never forget. Those special moments are the ones you need to cherish. By the way, those stuffed animals are nearly impossible to win." Paul is impressed.

Guilt seeps in and Trevor changes the conversation. "Listen, I know lately I've been a bear, but I want to let you know I appreciate our chats. Even though they aren't 'official' therapy sessions, after we hang out, I do feel better. I know sometimes you get on me, because you care, but in the end, you always seem to explain things in a way that resonates with me. It's not easy to air all my dirty laundry, even to you." Trevor leans against the edge of the pool table. "I really need to figure out how to fix things with Stacey. When we fight and argue, it feels like trying to walk in a straight line during an earthquake. I'm off kilter. Mentally, it's like going through a carwash with the windows open."

"Well, you're in luck. I happen to have the secret to fixing marriages, friendships...hell, even preventing wars. God knows marriage can feel like you're on a battlefield sometimes, right?" Paul takes a swig of his beer.

Trevor is deep in thought from that claim. "I don't know—your 'fix it' solution sounds too good to be true: like those book covers with rays of light reflecting onto a jewel that rests on an ancient map. If what you're about to say is true, let's bottle this secret and sell it. We could make a fortune. So, spill the beans: what is it?"

"Relax, man. It's nothing revolutionary. In fact, it's one of the most simplistic thought processes you could imagine. Let me ask you this question: why do most people argue and fight?" Paul leans over the pool table.

Trevor uses logic and replies, "I guess because they don't agree on whatever they're fighting about."

"And..." Paul encourages more to the answer.

Trevor folds his arms and stares at the ground. "I'm stumped. Go ahead and give me a failing grade on this one."

"Ahhh, you're so close." Paul pauses for a few seconds. "Yes, when people argue it's because they don't agree on something. Now, the fuse that keeps the fire burning is that each person wants to be right. Let's be honest with this next question. How great does it feel when the person you're fighting with apologizes and admits they were wrong?"

Trevor stands up straight and grins. "Are you kidding me? It feels awesome. Especially when I know I am right." Trevor looks around and whispers to Paul. "Which is almost all the time."

"Well, that's a big problem right there. You need to get over yourself." Paul flicks Trevor's earlobe and instructs, "Write down what I'm about to say." Trevor swipes to the memo function on his phone and is attentive. "What's more important, being right, or peace?" Paul doesn't wait for Trevor's answer, and he elaborates: "Now, I'm not suggesting to be someone's doormat, but ask yourself, is it *really* worth it? Does being *right* give you any long-term benefit?"

Trevor feverishly takes notes. He looks up at Paul. "That makes sense. I guess when Stacey and I get into an argument, I'm so emotionally charged, I have to win." Trevor paces and rubs his temples. "It's like I immediately go to a place in my mind where I need to corner her into agreeing with me. I don't let up. Now that I think about it, that's the same thing with most confrontations in my life. Tell me, Doc, how do I break the cycle?"

Paul claps. "You know, self-awareness and personal reflection are things most people are never able to achieve. It takes mental growth and maturity to be able to do that. I have patients in their 70s who still have no clue how impolite they can be when speaking to people. They have gone decades blaming other people for their own unhappiness. Then they wonder why friends and family members don't want to be around them. The victim mentality is an easy trap to fall into. I'm proud of you, Trevor. It's not easy for people to admit their shortcomings."

"I'm so desperate to get out of this funk, I'll admit anything at this point." Trevor acknowledges, "I guess I need to stop being the victim."

Paul jokes. "Dude, if I were teaching my psychology class right now, you would win student of the week. You're spot on. When people wear the *victim hat...*" Paul makes air quotations, "what they're really saying is they no longer have control of their own life. I get it: life is like a rollercoaster. Sometimes there are many circumstances we can't control, but identifying and choosing our best available options are how people keep moving forward. That's how we rediscover joy. It's also how we stop leaning on 'other things' for happiness." Paul makes his point about Trevor's social media dependency, and winks.

Trevor looks at his phone then tosses it across the pool table.

"Yo! No throwing things in here!" Trevor and Paul turn around, anxious to see who is shouting. They chuckle and reply in unison, "Boochman."

A tall, obese man walks over. His stomach protrudes from under his shirt. He high-fives Trevor and then Paul. "What are you girls up to? Damn, it's been a while. I don't think I've seen either of you since the gym closed. That must have been three years ago." Boochman uses a handkerchief to wipe beads of sweat from his forehead.

"Did you run a few laps in the parking lot, bud?" Trevor looks around and shouts, "Can someone get an oxygen tank over here?"

Boochman takes cover in the corner. "What's wrong with you? People are going to think you're serious. I'm a little out of shape; you don't have to rub it in."

That's Vincent Boochman. From as far back as I can remember, he's looked 10 years older than he was. Paul and I met Booch in fourth grade. He was the tallest kid in every class picture and could grow a full beard by his freshman year of high school. He was a gentle giant; that's the only reason I could get away with teasing him. He could crush me like a soda can if he wanted to, but it wasn't his demeanor. Booch was always heavy-set, but I was shocked to see how obese he became. The poor guy looked like he was one breath away from a heart attack. But that still wouldn't stop me from cracking a joke about his weight.

"Jeez, pal. Please don't pass out: I'm not sure they make reinforced stretchers." Trevor slaps his own knee.

Booch leans on the pool table and catches his breath. "You're a funny guy, Huxley. What can I say? A lot of stuff has happened in my life since the last time we all saw each other."

Paul senses some heartache and asks, "You OK, Booch? What's going on?"

"Do you have any open appointments, Doc? I'd need a couple of hours to go through my list. Where do I start?" Booch sits on a stool and lights up a stogie. "Well, for starters, I went back into an outpatient rehab program a few months ago. Every day is a struggle."

Booch stares at Paul's beer with resentment. I have full-blown diabetes and started insulin shots last month. I'm a ticking timebomb."

Trevor puts his repertoire of jokes aside. "Sorry to hear that. I'm sure it's not easy. How's the rehab going?"

"Not good. I haven't told you guys the worst part: two years ago, my nephew, Chase, was in a horrific car accident. He was in ICU for over two weeks. My sister and my brother-in-law had to make the decision that no parent should ever be faced with." Tears well up in Booch's eyes. "Ever since Chase passed away, my life has spiraled out of control. He was like a son to me. Speaking of which, you both know, I never got married or had my own kids. I've been single all of my life. When I was younger it didn't bother me, but lately it's downright depressing. It's no fun walking into a dark empty house, eating dinner by myself, and waking up alone. So, that's why I look like I do. Guys, I've been through hell and back since the last time I saw you."

Paul places his hand on Booch's back. "I'm proud of you, man."

"You're proud of me?" Booch isn't sure how to take that compliment.

Paul clarifies, "Yes. I'm proud of you. Do you realize how difficult it is for most people to talk about their life challenges? Even though we *all* experience trauma, society still looks at mental health in two buckets: the sick people and the healthy people. We all live on a mental health continuum." Paul takes the billiards rack and places it over his pool stick. He slides the rack from one side of the stick to the other. "Sometimes we're thriving, sometimes we're gliding, and hell, sometimes we are just surviving. Things are gonna get better, Booch. I'm here if you ever need to talk."

Trevor rubs his eyes and looks at Paul. "I wish I had that demonstration on video. How you explained that 'continuum thing' is spot on. There's years I was flying high and others I felt like I couldn't get off the ground."

Booch is shocked by that comment. "Wait a minute. You've struggled, Huxley? Every single time I see your social media posts, you're happy as a clam. Your wife and kids are *always* smiling." Booch's perception is sincere. "You have a beautiful family. Clearly, you're doing well at the office. I saw your post about that insane fish aquarium you bought. I can't even imagine how much that entire set-up was. It must have cost you thousands. Dude, you got the dream life. Who are you kidding?"

Trevor grabs his phone. "Uh, thanks, Booch. I do OK. Everyone goes through tough times. I give you credit for talking about it. I'm sorry to hear about everything you've been going through." Trevor sighs. "Too bad life isn't like the old days...back in high school. I remember our biggest stress was hoping we didn't get caught by Leo when we would cut class."

"Oh, shit! I remember Leo." Booch shares his memories. "He was the security dude who wore the aviator sunglasses and drove the golf cart around campus. I always loved that guy. You know something, I have a feeling he left the parking lot gate open so we could go to Bagel Land. It's like he knew we were just being kids and having fun. Those were great times, guys. We had no *real* worries or responsibilities. No one was trying to impress anyone. We didn't care what anyone thought of us, because we had each other." Booch takes a puff from his inhaler and wipes away a lingering tear.

Paul's intentional cough gets Trevor's attention. "Did you hear that, Huxley? We-didn't-care-what-anyone-thought-about-us, because we had each other: real-life friends."

The lights hanging above the billiard tables flicker off. An employee shouts from the back of the room, "Hey, guys, we're shutting it down!"

Booch looks at his watch. "Well, that sucks. The fun police had to spoil our reunion. It's the first time I've enjoyed myself in a *long* time." Booch bear-hugs Trevor and Paul. "It was awesome catching up with you dudes. Let's not wait another three years to do it again."

Trevor holds up his phone. "How about a picture for the road?" The crew huddle together and place their arms on each other's shoulders. "On three: one…two…Bagel Land!" The men laugh and Trevor snaps the photo.

The next morning:

Trevor pours pancake batter onto a sizzling skillet and then fills two glasses with fresh-squeezed orange juice. He dices up some fresh fruit.

"What are you doing up so early? I heard banging down here." Stacey walks into the kitchen.

Trevor flips the pancakes over. "Sorry, I was digging through the cabinet, trying to find the pan. I knocked over everything."

"Typical. Who are you cooking for? What's going on? Am I missing something?" Stacey can't imagine why Trevor is preparing an elaborate breakfast.

The aroma from the pancakes fills the kitchen. Trevor is careful as he uses his spatula to remove his masterpieces from the skillet.

"You can't tell me those aren't perfect flapjacks right there." Trevor kisses his fingertips like an Italian chef.

Stacey peers over Trevor's shoulder and compliments his work. "Not bad. The kids will be happy when they wake up."

"Good. They're still sleeping." Trevor rummages through the kitchen and looks for silverware and plates. He opens the last cabinet and exclaims, "Victory!" He rushes to set the table and transports the savory breakfast. "This isn't for the kids, Madam. Trevor tries to imitate his best French accent. "Come over and sit down with me."

Stacey's eyes widen. "Aren't those the porcelain plates we got for our engagement gift from your grandmother? I don't think we've ever used them before. Whoa, I didn't remember we had such nice silverware. What the heck are you up to? This whole *ordeal* seems suspicious. I don't know what got into you, but thanks for doing this."

"No need to thank me. I just felt like it. There's no hidden agenda, I promise." Trevor smiles and prepares a plate full of food for his wife. "I hope you like it."

Stacey relishes the moment. "What time did you get home last night? I never heard the garage door open."

"I didn't want to wake you up. I parked in the driveway and tiptoed inside the house through the front door. I was shocked that we closed the joint down. Before I knew it, we were getting kicked out. Oh, you won't believe who we ran into." Trevor can't wait to disclose the mystery guest.

Stacey wastes no time with her answer: "Boochman?"

Trevor drops his fork onto the table. "How the heck did you know that?"

"Hmmm, let's see…maybe because I checked Facebook before I came downstairs. It's a cute photo of you guys. I was shocked you posted a picture with friends. I can't remember the last time you did that. How's Booch doing? I don't want to be mean, but he looked pretty rough. Is everything OK with him?"

Trevor takes a deep breath. "Let's just say he's had a tough stretch over the last few years. You know, it's crazy to think that when we walk past someone, we have no idea what struggles they're going through. I could not believe how much he opened up to Paul and me. It was like a pressure cooker. Booch was ready to blow his top off. Once he started to talk about all the trauma he's been through, I could see his entire demeanor change. It was like all the steam evaporated into thin air."

"That makes sense. Sometimes talking about our feelings can be the best therapy. You know…being honest about our reality?" Stacey smirks.

Trevor swallows his food and asks, "Hey, what is that supposed to mean?"

"Never mind. I don't want to get into it. It will only lead to World War III. So, what's going on? Why all of this?" Stacey looks at the feast. "You haven't cooked me breakfast since the kids were born."

Trevor picks through the fruit bowl and puts all the pineapple onto a plate. He slides it in front of Stacey. "I just felt like doing something nice for you."

"Well, this is certainly a sweet gesture, but I'm more impressed with something else." Stacey's smile has Trevor curious.

Dumfounded, he looks around. "I'm stumped. What did I do?"

"You left your best friend charging on your desk upstairs." Stacey throws an intentional jab.

Trevor catches onto the subtle insult and debates his response. "You're still my best friend."

Stacey's eyelashes flutter. "Come on, that's not even believable. You can't stand me. You've told me *a million* times how much I annoy the shit out of you."

"I haven't been happy for a while. Maybe I've taken it out on you." Trevor places his hand on top of his wife's hand. "I don't know what's happening, but the last few days have been weird. Between my hangout therapy sessions with Paul and running into Boochman last night, I started to do some self-reflecting. Just don't tell anyone. I have a reputation to uphold." Trevor jokes and peers around to make sure the coast is clear. "It was heartbreaking to hear about everything Boochman has been through. The worst part was when he spoke about walking into an empty home: no one there to talk to about his day. No children yelling back to him and smearing toothpaste all over the bathroom." Trevor and Stacey chuckle at that mental picture. "I hate to say it, but sometimes you have to hear the heartache of someone else to appreciate the blessings of what's in front of you."

"Um, where's my husband and what did you do to him?" Stacey is stunned by Trevor's unexpected revelations.

Trevor hears thundering footsteps and looks up at the ceiling. "They're up."

Olivia and Luke race down the staircase and barge into the kitchen. They load their plates with food. Luke squirts syrup onto his pancakes and the kitchen counter. Trevor and Stacey can't hide their smirk.

Chapter Eleven

Mall Therapy

T revor laughs. "Whoever thought we would be part of the morning mall-walker clan? We're officially old." Paul and Trevor stare ahead at the group of senior citizens outpacing them. "Man, it's crazy: I can't believe how empty the mall is. Remember in high school, we could drive around for 20 minutes looking for a parking spot?" Trevor points at the abandoned store front. "Hey, that used to be Myron's video arcade. I would kick your ass in Mortal Kombat and NBA Jam. We would spend hours there."

Paul plays dumb with his response: "I don't know what you're talking about, but you know what I do remember?"

"What, you hitting on Stephanie Roebach next to the fountain in the food court? Ah, it seems like yesterday I was eating my warm slice of Sbarro pizza as I watched you get shot down." Trevor pretends to shoot a rifle into the air.

Paul isn't fazed by that insult and picks up his pace. "Yeah, well, you gotta swing the bat to hit a home run. The difference between us is I never cared what other people thought about me." Paul gears up to drop an unexpected bomb. "Since you want to bring up Stephanie

Roebach, we actually hooked up in college at a frat party. See, I never had to flaunt my accomplishments."

"Wait a minute, you hooked up with Stephanie? She was the hottest girl at our high school." Trevor gathers his composure. "I can't believe you never mentioned this to me over the last 25 years. I'm officially jealous!"

Paul provides some prospective. "There's nothing to be jealous about. My only reason for mentioning it was to try and convey that not everything needs to be shared or discussed. You can keep special memories in here." Paul points to Trevor's heart and keeps the conversation moving. "What I was going to say before you brought up Stephanie was you've always been obsessed about how other people perceive you. Speaking of the mall, I'll never forget you dragging me to Merry-Go-Round because you couldn't wear the same color Z Cavaricci's in the same week. Or the time you went into a depression because Josh Linkletter made fun of your Aspen cologne in front of the class. The best was when you played hooky, because you were afraid Boochman would tease you about riding your little brother's bicycle. You should be grateful they didn't have social media in the 1990s. God only knows what you would have posted back in high school."

"Awesome. I didn't know it was Insult Sunday. Thanks for making me feel like a loser. This was definitely the pick-me-up I needed. I guess we can't all be as *well-adjusted* as you are." Trevor doesn't take kindly to the barrage of embarrassing memories.

Paul holds up his hand as a sign to stop walking. "There are no insults, and I'm far from well-adjusted. I have my own issues like everyone else. What do you think, that because I appear to have it all together, I do?" Paul places his hands on Trevor's shoulders and gets personal. "What if I told you there were multiple times in my life when I had suicidal ideations? Thankfully I never acted on those urges. I was able to lean on a trusted colleague for support. Yoga and breathing therapy help keep my stress level down. I'm also on a low dose of an anti-anxiety medication. Listen, I'm not immune to mental health challenges."

"I'm not sure I can take any more bombshells today. First, I find out about you and Stephanie hooking up, and now you're telling me that you also struggled with your mental health." Trevor clasps his fingers behind his head and paces.

Paul clarifies, "I still struggle, Trevor. I am telling you this because I want you to understand that being self-aware is a great attribute, but making the actual behavior changes to improve your life is critical. The truth starts with you first. Once that happens, then you can decide on what comes next."

Trevor spots massage chairs and eases into one. "You know what feels like the biggest punch in my gut?"

Paul sits next to Trevor and is curious. "What is it?"

"When I run into people I don't see often and they think I have the 'perfect' life. Talk about guilt. Hell, I'm not even honest with you half the time." Trevor gets emotional and comes clean. "Dude, you know almost every post I make on social media is manipulated in some way. It's like a part of my content has some truth to it, but I'm not showing people what's really behind the curtain."

Paul performs the classic separating thumb trick and then looks for Trevor's reaction. "Like an illusion."

Trevor is surprised by the spot-on analogy and agrees. "That's exactly what it is." Trevor musters the nerve to share something he's been contemplating. "I don't think I'll ever do it, but a part of me wants to just come clean on social media."

Paul responds without hesitation. "I think it's a genius idea. Do you even realize we're in an epidemic right now when it comes to social media? Nowadays, children grow up listening to their parents talk about what everyone is posting. Here's something that will blow your mind…and I'm not making this up: There was a *very* interesting social experiment performed last year at a top university about this exact topic." Paul sits up. "So, there were two control groups. Each person participating had to follow five people on Facebook—people they didn't know. One control group received content from people living their absolute best life. I mean, these were amazing posts…visiting exquisite vacation destinations, celebratory occasions with their partner, sailing on luxurious yachts. You get the point. This was *Lifestyles of the Rich and Famous* type of stuff."

Trevor rubs his chin as he gets lost in thought. "Sounds interesting. What about the other group of people participating in the experiment?"

"Well, the second group was fed *much* more relatable content. You know, like people venting about the Monday morning blues, rush-hour traffic, and their kids misbehaving."

Trevor can't hide his shock. "That sounds like the stuff I'd like to post, but no one would be interested. To be honest, that type of content would probably just depress people."

Paul gets comfortable and smiles. "Oh, how wrong you are, my friend. Let me explain and give you a little more context. This social experiment lasted for six weeks. Both control groups received two posts per day. Once the experiment concluded, both groups were interviewed by psychiatrists who specialize in social analytical behavior studies. These doctors are trained to identify and treat people who experience severe social-related challenges. Anyway, after the evaluations were complete, the studies were quite shocking. Every single participant in control group one, who viewed people living their best life, had a consistent diagnosis. The study showed these individuals were comparing their own daily experiences and interactions to the ones they were viewing on social media." Paul takes an intentional deep breath. "I'll cut to the chase, Trev. Every person in the first control group experienced some degree of depression. It was documented that one individual had experienced thoughts of self-harm. Let me clarify that this same person also lost their father during the study, but I can tell you that being in control group one compounded the trauma tenfold."

Trevor is shocked by that news. "That's wild. I never would have guessed that outcome."

"I'll bet the results from the second control group will shock you even more." Paul leans in and is eager to share. "Remember, that group was viewing real-life experiences: the unfiltered version of someone's day. The good, the bad, and the ugly. These results were staggering, in my opinion. Fasten your seatbelt." The climax builds and Paul shares those details. "Every single person in control group number two had a documented *decrease* in stress and anxiety. Multiple people stated during the interview process they felt a sense of belonging. Actually, the word 'tribe' was used. They could relate to the events they were viewing. The psychiatrist concluded this group finished with an all-around improvement in their mental health."

Trevor's eyes bulge and he presses his palm against his forehead. "Holy smokes! Good thing this wasn't a test, because I would have failed. To be honest, I never would have guessed that." Trevor ponders the details of Paul's dissertation.

"Do you want to fall out of your chair?" Paul grins and doesn't give Trevor the chance to answer. "Every-single-post that control group number one viewed was staged. Part of the experiment was to use top Photoshop professionals to create an alternate reality. No one traveled the globe, or sailed around the seas on a yacht. In fact, the people used in the photos weren't even real. They were made using computer-generated imagery. It was nothing more than a facade."

Trevor's mouth falls open. "Oh my God. That may be one of the craziest things I've ever heard. So, you're telling me people became depressed and their mental health deteriorated, because they viewed what they believed to be people living a 'perfect' life?"

Paul stands up and stretches. "What's a perfect life? That's the real question. I think every person has a different interpretation of what that means. The point of my telling you about this social experiment is twofold. There are a lot of people who use social media to fill in the gaps within their own life. This epidemic runs deep, but I'll keep it short and to the point. In many cases, people aren't getting the validation they need in their personal life. So, they lean on social media to try and compensate. That's why you see so many people showing off their accomplishments. They're looking for immediate gratification. Some good ol' fashioned applause. Then when someone likes or makes a positive comment on their post, it just perpetuates that same behavior." Trevor scratches his head and relates to Paul's explanation. "Then you have the flip side, like the social experiment I mentioned. The people viewing those posts believed that individual has more joy and happiness in their life than they do. It's a vicious cycle on both sides of the coin. That's why I say it's an epidemic. I call it the social slaughter. In many cases, the person posting the content and the person viewing it are inadvertently fueling each other's insecurities. Unfortunately, this can spiderweb into serious mental health challenges. I see it every day with my patients. It's hard to believe how many people mention social media during their session."

"I need a nap. I'm emotionally spent." Trevor rubs his eyes and yawns. "After listening to you today, maybe I've been trying to compensate for my own insecurities. I guess my lack of self-esteem has haunted me for years." Trevor's chin drops to his chest. "It's interesting: the other day Stacey and I connected for the first time in what feels like years. It was refreshing to have no tension between us."

Paul is surprised by that news, and jokes, "What did you buy her? A new luxury car? Actually, let me guess: designer shoes?"

"I just made her breakfast." Trevor stares off into the distance and fights the urge to cry.

Paul pats Trevor's back. "Let's get going, pal. It's been an intense discussion." The men walk in the direction of the exit.

A Social Illusion

Chapter Twelve

JUMP Gymnastics

"D ad, why are you parking?" Olivia is surprised by the untraditional occurrence.

Trevor shuts off the car. "I thought I'd watch you practice tonight. My phone is charged and I finally deleted a bunch of old apps and pictures. I told Mom I'd get video of you nailing some back handsprings and front tucks."

"Jeez, Dad. Get a new phone with some decent storage space, will you?" Olivia finds that comical and razzes her father. "Or you can stop taking so many videos and pictures for your social media."

Trevor's laugh is sarcastic. "OK, you got me on that one. I've been cutting back. I haven't posted anything in days. That's a big accomplishment."

"For you, I agree, that's impressive. So, what's the occasion?" Olivia is curious.

Trevor bites his nails and contemplates how to answer that question. "I don't know, sweetie. Maybe I'm trying to get my priorities in order. You can be an old fart like me and still not have your life figured out. Sometimes you have to sink before you realize how deep you've gotten. I know that sounds odd."

Olivia is still skeptical. "So, let me get this straight: you're going to watch my routine tonight and not go onto social media?"

"I promise. I pinky swear." Olivia plays along and Trevor looks at his watch. "Hey, let's get going. Your class starts in five minutes. Make sure your jacket is zipped up—it's getting cold outside." Trevor places Olivia's hood over her head and hugs her.

Chapter Thirteen

REDEMPTION

Two Months Later: At the Office

Hey, Trev. Keith is looking for you. He seemed a little agitated. Not sure what you did this time." Cliff wonders what transpired.

Trevor's caught off guard. "Are you serious? Keith and I walked to the train station together last night and he was in a great mood. I can't imagine what changed between now and then?"

Cliff pushes the dagger deeper. "Yeah, well, something must have happened 'cause he slammed his office door closed. You may want to knock before you go inside or run downstairs and grab him one of his favorite donuts from the café."

Sweat covers Trevor's palms. "Awesome. No one is more fun to be around than Keith when he's in a bad mood. I don't get it, Cliff. I've worked so hard to make sure every proposal was perfect this quarter. I've even taken my laptop and worked outside on the balcony during lunch." Trevor looks through the window. "Man, what a difference it makes to get some fresh air. I can focus so much better when I have a clear mind."

"I'm glad you clarified, because we thought you were sneaking over to the Redlight Tavern over on 43rd and 5th. We figured you were hustling people at the pool table. Listen, when you speak to Keith, just play dumb. Don't tell him I told you anything. I just didn't want you to be blindsided if he loses it on you." Cliff pats Trevor on the back and walks away.

Just as Trevor sits at his desk, Keith walks out of his office and approaches. "You got a few minutes?"

Trevor looks around and points to himself. "You want to talk to me?"

"Considering you're the only one sitting in this pod right now, that's a solid guess. You're on fire and the workday hasn't even started yet. Meet me in my office." Keith's impatient demeanor is a clear indication something has gone awry.

Trevor rocks back and forth in his chair as he contemplates his next move. He takes a sip of water and musters the courage to walk into Keith's office. Trevor knocks on the opened door and pokes his head inside.

"Hey, Keith. What's going on?" Trevor is timid as he walks in.

Keith points to the door. "Hey, can you close that for me and have a seat?"

"Sure. No problem." Trevor obliges.

"You want a soda? I put a couple of fresh cans in the fridge." Keith leans back and places his arms behind his head. "I also loaded the cabinets with chips and cookies."

Trevor resists the urge. "Thanks. I appreciate it. Last month I changed my diet. I'm trying to cut out as much sugar as possible. It's amazing how much better I feel. I can't believe I was drinking four or five cans of soda a day." Trevor is relieved he overcame that addiction. "I think all the caffeine was contributing to my headaches."

"I was going to say, you look like you've lost quite a few pounds. Good for you. I wish I had the willpower." Keith pats his plump stomach. "The stress always seems to give me a reason to keep eating unhealthy."

Trevor relates to that struggle. "I know what you mean. It's not easy. I'm trying to work on the things I can control. That's where I've been putting my effort as of late. It's interesting: since I've been eating healthier, mentally I feel better. More grounded. It's not taking me three hours to fall asleep anymore. I'm getting a better night's sleep."

"It's interesting you mention those improvements. That's what I wanted to chat with you about. I've noticed a monumental change since we had our last discussion about your performance. Even John mentioned something to me. It seems like you're running your life, not your life running you. Before I ever give kudos to someone, I always make sure the behavior is consistent. I think it's fair to say you've been delivering at a high level for a while now." Keith reaches across the desk and high-fives Trevor.

Trevor takes a deep breath and unbuttons his collar. "I'm gonna kill Cliff! He got me so wound up that the vein in my neck was pulsating. I don't believe it. He had me convinced you were furious with me for something I did."

"Ah, don't blame Cliff. I told him to mess with you a little bit." Keith can't contain his urge to laugh. "Come on, you know me. I have to razz you a little bit before I can give you a compliment."

Trevor's reply is heartfelt. "I have to admit, I'm a little tongue-tied right now. I know that sounds odd coming from me." Trevor soaks up the moment. "Thank you, Keith. I can't tell you how much

I appreciate the compliment. Especially, coming from someone I look up to and admire."

"Relax, Huxley. Complimenting me isn't going to get you any further. However, executing on your projects at a high level will." Keith reaches behind him and grabs a manila folder. "Like you have been doing. Listen, you've gone above and beyond the call of duty. You know I go to bat for my team members when it's deserved, and that's what I did. Yesterday, I received the approval from Human Resources on an off-cycle pay increase I submitted for you." Keith places the folder in front of Trevor and opens it. He slides two pieces of paper out. "The first document has all the details of the pay increase. Since you're a salaried employee, it's listed in one lump sum, even though it will be broken out by pay period."

Trevor looks at the pay increase and falls back into his chair. "I don't know what to say, Keith. My life has been a rollercoaster the last year. I'm grateful you stuck with me."

"I'd never give up on someone who wouldn't give up on themselves." Keith lets out a deep breath and discloses a personal story. "I don't talk about it often, but about three years ago I was on a trip with my family at Universal Studios. Out of nowhere, I started having panic attacks. It was like someone turned off a circuit breaker in my brain. Within a day, it was a struggle to get out of bed and brush my teeth. I tried to camouflage how I was feeling to my wife and kids, but the anxiety and depression escalated so fast that I had to get medical assistance. I'm grateful my wife convinced me to see a therapist, because I couldn't function. In the midst of my foggy depression, the decision to get professional support may have saved my life. I won't get into all the details, but I promised myself if I could ever recover, I would be open to sharing my story."

Trevor is flabbergasted by his boss's candid admission. "Wow. I never would have guessed that. You're the last person I would ever think struggled with mental health. You're always so composed and polished. I'm blown away, Keith."

"I'm exactly the type of person who struggles with mental health, because I'm human. I still have my bad days. Today, I know what to do when I feel stress and anxiety begin to sizzle. There are so many silent sufferers out there like I was. People tend to think that because they're problem solvers in their career, they can fix their own mental health challenges. Some situations are bigger than we can handle on our own." Keith's perspective resonates with Trevor. "There's nothing wrong with raising your hand and asking for help. Happiness is always worth fighting for."

Trevor thinks back to a previous discussion with his boss. "I remember a few months ago you mentioned the free therapy sessions that are baked into our insurance plan. I found it odd that you brought that up. I figured since you were a vice president, you went through a wellness training to support your associates. I never imagined you used those therapy sessions for your own benefit."

Keith places his hand on his chest and gets to the point. "I have nothing to hide and I hope no one on my team ever does, either. I've always believed that when someone asks how you're doing, you should answer them honestly. It's the only way we will ever be able to normalize the topic of mental health. As someone who manages people, it's critical I know how my team members are feeling. Remember: money and material possessions are nice, but physical and mental health are priceless." Keith slides the other document in front of Trevor. "This is a note from Elliot Goff, the president of Trans-Universal. He couldn't stop raving about how easy you made their whole transition process. He was quite candid and mentions in this letter that he lost his sister-in-law to breast cancer a few months before we signed the contract with them. Apparently, he was going through a tough time and you were able to alleviate some of his stress. These are the types of letters that transcend building a marketing campaign for a client. This is how you make a significant impact in someone's life. Congratulations, my friend." Both men stand up and shake hands.

> To say I was caught off guard by how open Keith was about his own mental health issues was an understatement. Here's why: When my generation was growing up, we learned what to do if we caught on fire: Stop, drop, and roll. We learned to say no to drugs. Our classroom evacuation plan was posted on the wall, so we knew the safest way to exit the building. I remember being taught the basics of CPR in case someone ever stopped breathing. We were prepared for all those events if they ever occurred. You know what we never learned and weren't prepared for? What to do if our mental health suddenly went out on us. We never learned how to navigate through thoughts of self-harm or suicidal

ideations. We never learned that it was normal to feel anxious and worried at times—something that today sounds basic. So, when I say I was surprised by how open Keith was about his mental health challenges, that's why.

As I began to thaw from the numbness I was living in, my life started to feel meaningful again. I was beginning to get the validation I had been searching for. The more authentic interactions I had with people in my life, the less I felt compelled to share it on social media. To be honest, I was starting to feel confident. Special moments, like the one with Keith, were a blessing and I was content to just share them with my close friends and family. I was gaining back my momentum.

The friendship therapy sessions with Paul felt like a mental bootcamp, but they helped me get to a point of clarity. I was no longer expending energy to justify my mistakes. I had reached a place of self-acceptance.

Before I could share the thrilling news about my raise with Stacey, there was something tugging at my heartstrings that I needed to make right.

A Social Illusion

Chapter Fourteen

Diamonds Are Forever

Pawn Land

Trevor pushes the buzzer at the entrance and peers through the metal bars behind the glass doors. He glances at his watch and waits. Through the intercom, the store owner gives the green light. "You can come inside." The lock disengages. Trevor walks in and is fascinated by the variety of items for sale.

"What brings you in today?" The owner, an elderly man, greets Trevor from behind the display cases.

Before Trevor answers, he imagines the guilt felt by everyone forced to abandon their sentimental possessions. "How are you doing? It's sad to see all these items that meant so much to people."

"My name is George, by the way. It's the toughest part of running this business, son. I've been here over 40 years and it never gets easier watching someone give up their family heirlooms or personal treasures. The worst part is most people never come back in to reclaim their belongings." The man sprays glass cleaner onto the display cases and wipes them dry. "I never got into this business for selfish reasons. It was just an honest way to make a buck. Heck, there's even times I won't charge a customer interest. I sell their item back for what I paid."

Trevor walks up to the counter. "That's nice of you. I'm sure people appreciate that."

"So, tell me, what can I help you with?" George takes his glasses from his shirt pocket and places them on his face.

In despair, Trevor shares his dilemma. "I made a big mistake in here a few months ago. I sold something I should have never parted with. I'm praying you still have it here."

George grabs a thick binder from the shelf. It's stuffed with invoices. He places it onto the counter. "Well, I can tell you if it's been months, chances are whatever we bought from you is long gone. What's your name?"

"It's Trevor. My last name is Huxley." Trevor crosses his fingers and paces.

George opens the binder and finds the tab labeled with the letter H. "Let's take a look-see in here. Some people laugh at me 'cause I never got into that computer stuff. I believe in good ol' fashioned bookkeeping. It's never let me down since I started this business."

"Technology has its good and bad, for sure." Trevor's patience begins to run thin.

George flips through each page looking for Trevor's invoice. "Speaking of technology, my granddaughters keep telling me I should start a business page on social media. What a stupid concept. The thought of having conversations with people I never met in person makes me cringe." George finds Trevor's invoice and continues his rant. "The way you build friendships or a business, is to look people in the eye and shake their hand. Then ask them questions about themselves. That's how you find similarities. You know, last week a wonderful couple came into the store. We talked for at least

30 minutes. I found out the woman's uncle was in the same fraternity as I was at Ohio State. This was back in the late 1950s. What were the odds? He's still going strong and lives in New Albany. The next time he comes here to visit his daughter, we're going to see each other. So, you see where I'm going with this? It breaks my heart to see my grandchildren waste so much time on that stupid thing." George points to Trevor's smart phone. "They should spend time building face-to-face relationships instead of sharing their two cents with people they never met. I'm sure most of what people write on social media is a fallacy, anyway. At least that's my opinion."

"You know, George, I have a feeling that's probably the truth. You're a smart man and I hope your granddaughter takes your advice." Trevor peers over at the binder. "So, any luck with my item?"

George clears his throat and explains, "I'm sorry. I tend to lose my focus quite easily these days. It's my attention deficit disorder. You know, I wasn't diagnosed until I was in my 70's. Can you believe I went most of my life not knowing why I couldn't remember what I had just read? High school was a disaster for me...and forget college. I didn't make it more than two years at Ohio State before I realized continuing my education was a waste of time and money." George gathers himself and gets back to the task at hand. "OK, Mr. Trevor Huxley, here's your invoice."

"Please, give me some good news." Trevor taps on the glass.

George takes his glasses off and frowns. "I'm sorry, son. Each month we consolidate the nicer jewelry people don't come back for and sell it to a local auction house. Nearby jewelers buy it and melt down the gold and re-mount the diamonds. Especially vintage pieces like the one you had."

Trevor clenches his fists and mutters, "Damn it."

A woman with gray hair in a bun walks through a door behind the counter. She looks at Trevor and tilts her head. "Well, you look quite familiar, young man."

Heartbroken, Trevor replies with a solemn tone, "Hi. You helped me a couple of months ago when I sold a ring. I came back in today hoping you still had it. I made a big mistake. I never should have sold it in the first place." Trevor shakes his head and processes the situation. "Now it's gone forever."

"Who told you we didn't have it?" The woman inspects the invoice.

Trevor looks at George and replies, "He did."

The woman picks up a clip board and pretends to hit George over the head with it. "Oh, don't listen to him. My husband would forget his head if it wasn't attached." The woman scolds George for the obvious mistake: "Jeez, George, come on. It says right there in the notes that I kept that one to sell in the showcase. It was such a beautiful ring there was no way I could send that off to auction. I'll be right back." George looks at Trevor with remorse and apologizes, "I'm so sorry."

Trevor points to the sky as acknowledgment of divine intervention. "No problem, George. It was only a minor heart attack. I should be OK."

"Here you go, sweetie." The woman hurries over and gives Trevor the ring. His hands shake as he inspects his grandmother's brilliant-cut, solitaire diamond. "I'll tell you why it's still here if you want to know the truth," the woman is eager to share.

Trevor is careful as he places the ring on the counter. "Yes, tell me. Why is it still here?"

"Because I knew you would come back for it." The woman polishes the ring and then places it inside a felt-lined box. "I priced that ring so high I knew no one would buy it. I could see the hurt in your eyes the day you came in." She pats Trevor's hand. "Settle up with George, honey. We aren't charging you any interest or fees. I'm just happy it's back in its rightful hands."

Trevor breathes lighter and closes his eyes. "Thank you."

Chapter Fifteen

Swoosh!

Littles Park

L uke shoots the basketball and misses the rim. "I swear, I'll never be able to make a shot, Dad." Luke trudges toward the bench.

"Well, with that attitude you won't. Come on, get back here and keep working on that shot. Remember what I taught you." Trevor demonstrates. "Guide the ball with your left hand and extend with the right hand. Elbow in and make sure you do the swan-neck finish with your wrist like I showed you. I'm in no rush today, pal. I told mom we would be at the park for at least an hour working on your shot." Trevor rolls the basketball to Luke.

Luke dribbles the ball and thinks about that comment. "Wait a minute. You're not in a rush? You're going to work on my shot with me?" Luke walks over and tugs on Trevor's ear.

"Ouch! What the heck was that for?" Trevor winces.

Luke whispers into his father's ear, "I had to make sure you weren't an alien wearing a mask that looks like my dad. What's gotten into you? Olivia told me and mom that you watched her entire gymnastics class…without checking your cell phone once. We're all concerned about you. I think we may need a family invention."

Trevor is amused by his son's stark humor. "You mean an intervention? That's a good one, though. I've told you and your sister before, just because I'm an adult it doesn't mean I can't try and be a better dad. I hope you and Olivia learn from my mistakes, because I'm not afraid to share them with you. I don't hide anything."

"How can someone tell when they need to be a better person?" Luke shoots the basketball and it rolls off the rim.

Trevor passes the ball to Luke. "That's a good question, bud. I guess my answer would be that it's when you keep letting down the people you love. You see, they might not tell you, but after a while you will notice. You have two choices when that happens: either you can ignore it or you look yourself in the mirror." Trevor clarifies. "That last line is an old expression. It means to be honest with yourself. It's not an easy thing for people to do, but when it happens, you can change your life for the better."

"Don't be so hard on yourself, Dad. No one's perfect." Luke shoots the ball and it ricochets off the backboard.

Trevor grabs the rebound and responds, "Thanks, Luke. I appreciate it. You're right: no one is perfect. Just do your best to acknowledge your mistakes and try not to repeat them. Other than that, enjoy being a kid. It's one of the best times in your life. I'm going to work hard to focus more of my time on you and Olivia. I need you guys to stay on me. If either of you see me pull out my phone, you have my permission to yell at me. It's a hard habit to break."

"You mean your kryptonite? Yeah, don't worry. Me and Olivia have a plan the next time you miss something that's important to us." Luke's scowl is playful and he holds up his fist.

Trevor backs away with his hands in the air. "OK, OK, you have my word. I promise. I wouldn't mess with someone who looks that angry."

Luke's wink shows he's got something up his sleeve. He snatches the basketball from Trevor and dribbles to the free-throw line. He gets into his shooting stance. Luke looks at his father and then stares at the rim. He launches the basketball into the air, it bounces on top of the rim, and drops through the net. Trevor cheers and Luke runs into his father's arms. "I love you, Dad."

Trevor places his palms onto Luke's face and looks him in the eyes. "I love you too, buddy. I love you, too."

Chapter Sixteen

Date Night

Tuscan's Bar & Grill

"Are you sure the kids will be OK? I feel guilty leaving them alone." Stacey struggles to unwind.

Trevor tries to calm his wife. "Olivia is 14 years old, babe. She's capable of keeping an eye on her brother so we can grab dinner. She has her phone and can call us if she needs anything." Trevor caresses Stacey's hand. "Relax. Let's just enjoy some alone time. It's been forever since we've gone on a date."

Stacey appreciates the moment. "I can't remember the last time. It feels like years ago. You know, it makes me sad sometimes. I think back to how much fun we used to have together. I wouldn't change anything—you know that—but sometimes it feels like Groundhog Day. We get up, snap into our routine, go to sleep, and then repeat it the next day. The years are rolling by like minutes. I can't even re-member when the kids were little anymore. It was like a blur."

"Is that your way of telling me you want another little Huxley baby?" Trevor grins and teases his wife.

Stacey is quick to clarify. "Not in a million years. Are you kid-ding me? We have our hands full and we were blessed enough to have a boy and a girl. Two wonderful kids. Not to mention, I'm a hundred years old now. So, no, I don't want any more children. I just want a glimpse of what we used to have. I think if we work hard at it, we can find that spark again. That is, as long as you don't want to trade me in."

"Come on, I'd never trade you in. You're stuck with me. The kids and I would be lost without you. I mean that. You're the reason they're so well adjusted. Your expertise is structure and sticking to a schedule. You have the discipline to read every single email about school and their extracurricular activities. I don't think I could get past the first sentence without losing interest. God only knows how unorganized the kids would be without you. Most important, I still love spending time with you."

Stacey's face is flush from all the compliments. "Well, thank you. Sometimes I feel like a failure. When I see the kids struggle, I think it's my fault—like I haven't done enough."

"You go above and beyond for our children. All kids are going to struggle at some point. It doesn't matter how great of a parent you are. It's like expecting a child to never have a cold. Unless you keep them inside a bubble, it's impossible for them not to catch one. And schools still aren't doing enough to support kids emotionally, either. As a society we're brainwashed into thinking academics is the foundation of a successful life. The truth is, there needs to be effective mental health programming layered into school curricula—a lot of it. It's more important than anything academically, in my opinion. It's time to ditch the useless information students are required to memorize and replace it with knowledge that helps them cope with life's challenges." Trevor's insight intrigues Stacey.

"You're making a lot of sense lately. It's not like you." Stacey and Trevor laugh at the understated, but accurate, insult. "It looks like all your play-dates with Paul are paying off."

Trevor explains, "It's funny you should say that. It ended up being a blessing to have a best friend who's a psychologist. It's kind of odd: I've known his profession for years, but was never interested in getting his insight. It's hard to believe how much he's been able to help me understand why I've been stuck in a rut for the last year. Even more important, he's coached me on how to reboot my life."

"I'm grateful he's been able to make you feel better. Paul has always been someone you could count on. Was there anything specific he helped you with?" Stacey checks her phone to see if the kids sent a text.

Trevor lines up his silverware and fidgets with his napkin. "I guess if I had to pick one thing, it was our discussions about social media. It's not easy for me to talk about. I've realized it was my outlet to help compensate for many of my insecurities. I've never told you how far down that rabbit hole went for me.

"I would never judge you, honey. I think the fact that you're able to recognize something like that is amazing. It's not easy for anyone to analyze themselves." Stacey holds Trevor's hand. "Listen, I have my own faults, too. We just need to be there for each other. At the end of the day, we're both doing the best we can. This parenting thing isn't easy, especially if you do it the right way."

Trevor thinks hard about that and rubs his eyes. "I agree with you. It's been a tough year. I appreciate you sticking with me and putting up with all my social media nonsense. I'm sure I drove you crazy."

"Well, I never said anything to you about it, because I thought posting about your life made you happy," Stacey replies with compassion.

Trevor shakes his head. "No, looking back now, it didn't make me happy. It gave me temporary relief, like a drug would. It gave me the validation I was desperate to find. I felt If I created an alternate life, one that appeared to be perfect to others, it would fill the voids in my own reality." Trevor's sigh signals a sense of relief. "It was exhausting to keep the façade going as long as I did. I've never even told you all the effort I put into manufacturing some of those mirage posts."

"Honey, I don't even want to know." Stacey's sarcastic tone hides her unease. "I'm the most private person in the world, so seeing you post our personal life on social media made my skin crawl. Especially when the kids and I would be part of the act. Let's just say if I made a top three list of what annoys me the most, your social media shenanigans would be number one. The fact is, Trevor, you've cared more about what strangers think about your life than what your own family thinks. I'm sorry, I didn't plan on discussing this tonight, but since you brought it up, it's how I feel."

Trevor's shoulders slump. "I'm the one who should be sorry. I got caught up in the social frenzy." Trevor stares at his phone. "When you're in the middle of the chaos, you don't realize the strength of the storm. Then once it's over, the ripple effects seem to run as wide as the Grand Canyon. I can't believe how much I went out of my way to try and impress people I have no real relationship with."

"The most important thing is you've come to that realization. Maybe you need a break? There's nothing wrong with that." Stacey holds Trevor's hands and stares into his eyes. "The kids and I love you more than anything. I don't care what car you drive or how much money is in our bank account. That stuff has never meant anything to me. Let's just try and live the best life we can together. That's all I want."

Trevor holds back tears. "I want that, too. You have my commitment. You know, now that all the dust has settled, I feel like the biggest idiot. The thrill I would get from someone acknowledging my content was like a rush of adrenaline. But it was fleeting."

"Stop beating yourself up. I can't tell you how many times I see my own friends post things that I know are misleading." Stacey lowers her voice. "Do you remember the time Beth posted the most heart-warming tribute to Jeff on their 10th wedding anniversary? She forgot to mention the fling she had with the bartender during the girls' trip to the Florida Keys. Or what about when Michelle posted pictures of the new mansion and wrote, *working hard to accomplish my dreams.* Her freakin' grandmother bought the house for her in cash. However, the best post of all time was when Cynthia bragged about her luxury designer handbag. I'll never forget this one. She posted a photo of herself standing underneath the storefront sign. The duck-lips pose and bag over her shoulder sold the moment, until I found out she paid 25 dollars for a knockoff. My hairdresser was selling them to everyone in town."

Trevor's mouth drops open and he places his hands on top of his head. "That is ab-so-lute-ly classic! I gotta give Cynthia credit: that beats any of my posts by a landslide. That's some impressive creativity."

"You better not say anything. Promise me, Trevor." Stacey second-guesses herself for spilling the beans.

Trevor has a devilish grin and rubs his hands together as a sign he's ignoring Stacey's plea. "I'm just kidding. I'm not going to say anything, but I need to call your hairdresser. I could use one of those bags. After all, your birthday is coming up soon."

"Honey, you know I'm the last person who cares about a designer bag. I've told you before, the way to this mama's heart is simple: ask me how my day was, hold my hand, or watch television with me. I'd say you have it pretty easy, Mr. Huxley. All those requests are free of charge." Stacey crosses her arms and waits for Trevor's response.

Trevor stares at Stacey and caresses her forearm. His lips quiver as he whispers, "I'm sorry." Stacey assures him, "I love you. Never forget that."

Chapter Seventeen

Awakening

April—The Oval

Trevor and Paul round the corner. Leaf buds burst from a massive oak tree's branches. The crisp morning breeze blows Trevor's hood off his head. He raises both his arms into the air and shouts, "I swear, days like this are the best! Man, I wish the weather was like this year-round." Trevor closes his eyes and raises his head toward the cloudless sky. Starbursts of light penetrate his eyelids.

Paul jokes, "You could always move to San Diego."

"You know, I used to think if I moved away from the Northeast, I'd be happier." Trevor shares his list of complaints: "Imagine, no more potholes and sidewalks that look like crumbled Oreos. I'd be able to say goodbye to icy windshields, snow-filled driveways, and puffy winter coats."

Paul puts life into perspective. "Yeah, but you'd be leaving behind the smell of spring, the rebirth of nature, and of course, coffee talk at the town pool. What about apple picking with the kids, roasting marshmallows in the fire pit, and all the small-town festivities? Isn't it interesting how often we dwell on the things we wish were different, instead of recognizing the blessings in front of us?"

Trevor raises his hand. "Guilty as charged, Your Honor. For some reason, my mind is like a radar. It's programmed to seek out the negatives in my life and then I try and fix them. Before I know it, I've exhausted years of effort, and gotten little in return."

Paul offers his perspective. "So, you said a key word: programmed. You've provided your mind with instructions to operate that way. It doesn't know any different. When something is programable and we are conscious of it, we can tap into that system and make the necessary adjustments to operate differently. We are in control. I've always used the analogy that our minds work like a television. We can watch a program that may make us scared or anxious, but once we have had enough, we just change the channel to a different network. Why not do the same thing with our thoughts?"

"Wow. You make it sound so easy." Trevor is baffled by the simplistic explanation.

Adding context, Paul continues, "It's not that easy. Don't beat yourself up. The human mind is powerful and complex. The greatest neuroscientists in the world still don't fully understand all the intricacies of the brain. For now, just try and keep it simple. Be aware of what you find yourself focusing on. Catch yourself. If it isn't something productive, do your best to change the channel. Try to steer your thoughts toward the light and avoid the darkness. You will know the difference. You'll feel it in your gut."

"See, if I ever moved away, I wouldn't have these friend-sessions." Trevor pats Paul's back. "What you just said about light and darkness, can you clarify what you mean by that?"

Paul points at the bench. "Let's take a little break and I'll explain." The men get comfortable. "So...people exude energy. I believe our souls are molecules of light. Some souls shine brighter than others. Every now and then you'll find one where the light switch doesn't work." Paul pauses to gather his thoughts. "Let me ask you this question. Have you ever gotten to know someone and you could feel the warmth in their aura?"

"I have. There's a glow to them. You're right. It's almost like I can feel their energy," Trevor explains.

Paul nods. Those are the people you want to be around. The warmth of those individuals is like soup for the soul. Like rays of sunshine. You know, we spend way more time thinking than doing." Paul taps the top of Trevor's head. "So, make sure those thoughts are about people that bring you light and energy, not people who take it from you."

Trevor soaks in the advice and offers a compliment: "I don't know how I would have gotten through the last six months without you, man. I can't believe you never shared all this knowledge years ago."

"You never asked. I'm not one to offer unsolicited advice." Paul's posture stiffens. "Well, I do make some exceptions to that rule." The men get up and continue on their stroll. "Listen, it sounds like you've got a mental tug-of-war going on. In my humble opinion, I think it's the guilt of all your social media trickeries. I can tell it still bothers you."

Trevor pretends to throw a dart. "Bullseye. Are you sure Stacey isn't feeding you intel on the side? I'm starting to get a complex that you two are in cahoots. It's like you know me better than I know myself."

"Not really. You've opened up and told me what's on your mind. I wish all my patients did that. Oh, by the way your bill is in the mail." Paul's joke stirs laughter. "Sometimes it's like pulling teeth to get people to let their guard down. I've learned the most difficult challenge for people is to say the words 'help me.'"

Trevor thinks back to the whirlwind of events from the previous year. "I can understand why. The entire process of finding a doctor is usually based on who will accept the patient's insurance. It's a broken system, because when it comes to mental health, having a connection with the doctor is critical. Then once you find a doctor, you get to fill out a bundle of paperwork with the most frightening questions possible." Trevor works hard to articulate his points. "The receptionist calls out the patient's name and then comes the walk of shame. The door marker labeled *Clinical Psychiatrist* makes the patient feel even more stressed. Once the patient walks into the office, they see all the fancy degrees and accolades plastered all over the wall. I swear, it can make you feel worthless. My favorite part is the bookshelves filled with titles about every disorder ever named. This way you can get a preview of all the disorders you could be diagnosed with. Then by the time you hit the tweed couch, you're drained."

Paul jokes, "OK, I think I need my own therapy session after that mental voyage to the doctor's office. I pray someone never gives me a review like that. If I'm being serious, you're right. There's still a stigma associated with seeing a mental health specialist. What you just described is why so many people don't get the mental health support they need. That 'Sigmund Freud' approach to therapy is antiquated, with the dimly lit office and couch. Today, people don't want a disorder diagnosis, they want relief. In my opinion, being put into a category just isolates people even more." Paul looks at his watch. "I have to get going soon, but I'm curious, do you know someone who went through what you described? You don't have to tell me who it is."

Trevor places his elbow on Paul's shoulder. "Yeah, me. I took your advice and went for a couple of sessions back in December. My insurance covered the cost, but it had to be in network. So, I was left with one option—a therapist older than my grandmother. She reminded me of Dorothy from the show *Golden Girls*. She handed me a list of five possible mental health disorders I might be suffering from. Her office smelled like mothballs. Trevor pinches his nose closed. "Needless to say, I stopped going to see her."

"Oh boy. So, you gave me a play-by-play of your own experience, but tell me how you've been feeling lately? I can't remember the last time you posted something on your social media." Paul wonders what triggered the extreme behavior change.

Trevor's posture softens. "I'm feeling much better. My thoughts are clearer. Like you said before, I'm still struggling with guilt about how I manipulated my online posts. I feel like I photoshopped my life." Trevor places his hand on his stomach and slouches. "I feel nauseous just talking about it. I keep thinking back to all the times someone commented about how great my life seemed."

"This is a bold suggestion and I know we've joked about it before, but I think you should consider coming clean on Facebook. If the guilt is bothering you as much as you're saying, post something about it. You don't need to write an autobiography, just figure out in your own way how to get the message across. It will help you close the book on this last chapter and maybe help someone else in the process." Paul's reply resonates in several ways.

Trevor bites his fingernails. "Do you think I should make a video or just write something? Maybe I could post an article related to how I'm feeling now?"

"I can't answer those questions. When the time is right, you'll know what to do. I gotta roll. Give me a call later." Paul jogs toward his car and Trevor waves goodbye.

Chapter Eighteen

A Social Reality

Disney World — Trevor's Birthday

"D ad, can I get a snack? I'm starving!" Luke licks his chops as he stares at the concession stand.

Trevor asks Stacey for the green light. "What do you think? Should I grab him something to eat? Popcorn or cotton candy?"

"This would be his *third* snack, plus I'm sure he'll want birthday cake later—and the parade will be starting soon. We have to get to Main Street early if we want to grab a good place to sit. You know how fast the sides of the street fill up with people." Stacey takes out her phone and clicks on the park application. She swipes through screens. "OK, I checked the map, and we're only 10 minutes away. That's fine…go ahead, but try and hurry up, please."

Trevor looks at Stacey and salutes. "Yes, ma'am. He turns to his daughter. She's wearing Minnie ears. "Olivia, do you want anything, princess? I think they have those *gigantic* Mickey Mouse lollipops you like."

"Ooh, yes! I'll have one of those, please. Thanks, Dad." Olivia smiles in anticipation of the sugar rush.

Trevor dashes over to buy the treats. Stacey and the kids huddle. "Luke, great job, although for you it's not acting. Olivia, he went for the Mickey Mouse lollipop on his own, but way to keep a straight face." Stacey compliments the kids and they high-five. "Guys, now is the time. Let me call Uncle Jordan."

"Do you think Dad will be surprised, Luke?" Olivia wonders as she sees Trevor in the distance.

Luke is impatient. "Duh, of course he will."

"OK, guys, I spoke to Uncle Jordan. Everything is set. When your father walks up, act normal. Pretend you're excited about your snacks or something." Stacey stands on her tippy toes and shields the sun with her hand. "I see him heading back."

Trevor walks steadily as he tries to balance his tray full of snacks and drinks. "Alright, everyone. The snack bar had to close, because I bought everything."

Luke's critique is harsh: "That is *such* a terrible dad joke."

"Geesh, babe. What the heck *did* you buy?" Stacey peers over at the tray.

Trevor's proud of his excursion finds. "I bought you a lemon icy and snagged a couple of sodas and pretzels. I managed to grab the last popcorn and didn't forget about Olivia's lollipop."

"Well, I guess it's a good thing you brought a few extra snacks and drinks. Close your eyes." Stacey bubbles with anticipation.

Trevor sets down the tray, shuts his eyes and asks, "What are you up to, Babe? Luke, Olivia, help me out here." The kids whistle and look away.

"Oh, would you just listen to me and keep your eyes closed?" Stacey smacks Trevor's rear-end and he obliges. She places her hands on Trevor's shoulders and turns him in the opposite direction. "OK, so *do not* open your eyes until I say to."

Trevor's nervous laugh defines the awkward moment. Stacey points at her kids as an indication to start the countdown. In unison, they begin: "One, Two, Three!" Trevor's eyes flash open and he stands frozen. Trevor's brother, Jordan, pushes a wheelchair toward him with their grandmother seated comfortably. She kisses her fingertips and blows a kiss. Trevor glances past his grandmother and recognizes two men walking behind Jordan. They make eye contact. One man fist pumps and barks like a dog, the other man responds with an understated wink and wave.

"What-is-going-on?" Trevor clasps Stacey's forearm and places his hand on his chest. "I don't believe this is happening." Paul and Boochman stand on each side of Trevor's grandmother. The crew claps and sings an off-key rendition of the Happy Birthday song. Trevor is overcome with emotion as goosebumps cover his arms. After Boochman elongates the last note in the song, Trevor addresses his friends and family: "I don't know what to say. I feel like this isn't real." Trevor points to Jordan and asks, "When the heck did you fly down?"

Jordan gives the backstory. "Well, you can thank your *amazing* wife. She arranged this entire surprise months ago. I mentioned it to Grandma and she couldn't wait to get down to the Sunshine State. We landed this morning and took an Uber to the park. It was a smooth trip."

Trevor hugs Paul and high-fives Boochman. "OK, you two. It's time to let the cat out of the bag. How did you guys pull this off? Especially, you, Paul. I just saw you two days ago."

"I'm good at keeping secrets and I knew Stacey would have kicked my ass if I messed this up." Paul's answer is sincere.

"So, Booch, you flew down here just for me?" Trevor feels flattered.

Boochman sets the record straight. "I love you, buddy, but not that much." He laughs and rubs the top of Trevor's just-styled hair. The truth is my company just wrapped up a three-day conference in Clearwater, so I stayed an extra night and drove over. The timing was perfect. I also wanted to share some good news in person with you. The night I ran into you and Paul at the Landmark..." Booch tears up. "It changed the trajectory of my life. You guys were the first people I spoke to about my mental health in years. It was like an old blackhead squeezed out of my back. The relief was exhilarating." Everyone shows their distaste for that analogy and groans. "Sorry, bad joke, but kind of true. Anyway, I ended up making an appointment with this guy." In a juvenile fashion, Booch pretends to kiss Paul's cheek. "And six months later, I'm now able to get through a day without crying. I've even been dating again."

"Whoa! Paul, you never told me Booch was your patient." Trevor tries to process the news.

Paul explains, "There's something called HIPAA laws, but since Booch disclosed it on his own...yup, he's been my patient." Paul's admiration for Booch is evident by his smile. "I couldn't be prouder of him."

A Disney tour guide frolics over. Her digital camera hangs around her neck and she holds a megaphone. The cheery woman reaches into her flare-covered vest and takes out a small pad. She glances at the scribbled notes. Her enthusiastic announcement stops park patrons in their tracks. "I hear we have an important birthday we're celebrating today!"

Another Disney employee, dressed in a Mickey Mouse costume, marches out of the gift shop. Mickey hugs Olivia and Luke and then places his arm around Trevor.

Trevor whispers to Stacey, "You got Mickey Mouse to come to my birthday celebration? I'm in heaven."

The tour guide speaks into her megaphone and directs the group in preparation of the special keepsake. "OK, I need Mickey in the middle, standing next to the birthday boy. Everyone else please fold in around them. Squeeze together the best you can. Mickey doesn't bite, unless you steal his cheese." A faint courtesy chuckle echoes from the group. "I need you all to say *Happy Birthday, Trevor,* when I say the word, 'Mickey.'"

Everyone scrambles into position for the photo op and poses. Booch can't resist the urge to lean over and use his fingers to give Trevor rabbit ears. The tour guide shouts the code word, 'Mickey!'

After the photograph, Trevor faces Stacey and places his hands on her shoulders. He recalls the depths of his depression and gazes into her eyes. His words are soft spoken, but sincere: "Thank you."

Tears well in Stacey's eyes. "For what?"

Trevor kisses his wife's forehead. "For never giving up on me."

> It's fascinating how the crossroads in our lives can lead us to the moments we cherish forever. That day felt perfect. I was with my friends and family, the people who love and care about me. My cup was full and I was grateful to feel the spark that

triggered my joy and happiness again. I was firing on all cylinders. Don't get me wrong, it was a slow climb out of the abyss. I made a conscious effort to reprogram my mind and started to believe there was light at the end of the tunnel.

As for coming clean on social media, I did. It was a bit more subtle than I anticipated, but it felt right. I shared that photograph at Disney World and I wrote nothing. I knew it was the first authentic post I made in years and that's what mattered.

There is a lesson to be learned in every situation. For me, it was the realization that in the world of social media, most people are posting their highlight reel. You're viewing the best moments of their life. It's important to be happy for other people, but also realize you're only seeing a glimpse into their reality. Don't waste valuable time comparing your life to someone else's, for sometimes what you see may be nothing more than a social illusion.

The End

Epilogue

W hen writing, I tend to create characters inspired by people and circumstances in my own life. For example, I can recall my daily commutes into Manhattan. Every day was an adventure, with endless writing material at my fingertips.

If you've ever made that trek from North Jersey during rush hour, you know it could be a two-hour delight. I often wondered what people did to kill time 15 to 20 years ago: Read the newspaper? Listen to their Walkman? Stare at the New York City skyline? Lucky for my generation, we have our smart phones.

Prior to 2013, I wasn't interested in social media. In fact, I remember my wife teaching me what a direct message was and how to make a post. Once I understood those details, I recall thinking, man, this is amazing! I can find friends I lost contact with and send them a message. Even though I hardly had a minute to catch my breath, all I had to do was tap on my social media apps and there it was: I knew everything that was going on in my friends' and families' lives. I thought, *this could be the most powerful resource the world has ever seen.* So, I'll bet you could imagine how I passed the time during my commute for the next six years. Yup, checking my social media.

Over the course of that time, I found the content I was scrolling through didn't always correspond with what I was seeing or hearing in my 'real' life. For example, I would see photos of a couple that looked blissful, but I heard through the grapevine that they were on the verge of divorce. I recall seeing an acquaintance asking for recommendations on a luxury item, but I knew her spouse lost his job and was borrowing money to keep the lights on. Yes, gossip flew around my town faster than an F-15. The post that shook me more than usual was a specific selfie of my friend. This individual was smiling from ear to ear, despite telling me the same day she was depressed. I began to wonder why people would feel the need to portray something that wasn't accurate on social media. What are they seeking...or more accurately, what are they missing?

Hearing chatter around town about how perfect another person's life seemed, based on their social media posts, became a daily occurrence. I started to question: why would someone compare their life to another person's social media posts, especially if there was a chance that what they saw was a mirage?

I wanted to acknowledge the power source that connects the world, which is social media. Because of this platform, millions of relationships have been forged or rekindled. It's something worth celebrating.

For most, social media is the place where we share the highlights of our lives. The moments we often wish we had back. But what if we could also leverage social media to be a place where we felt comfortable sharing our difficult moments? Since we all go through challenges, why not use social media to be a platform where we could say, *I'm really struggling today and could use some support?*

I was purposeful in making sure almost every character you met spoke about their mental health challenges. It was critical to show, despite our different outcomes, that the traumas we face impact our nervous systems in a similar manner. This is what makes us able to relate to each other's experiences.

I hope this story helps to change society's perception of social media and continues to open up the discussion around mental health.

Acknowledgements

Thank you to my friends and advisors, without whose assistance **A Social Illusion** could not have been produced.

- Dr. Andrew Greenberg. Friend and the inspiration for the character Paul Mintz

- Eric Kussin. Founder and CEO of #SameHere – The Global Mental Health Movement

- Heidi Newman, my editor

- Dr. Andrew Pleener, Integrative Psychiatrist

- Adam Shapiro. My brother and the inspiration for the character Jordan Huxley.

- Peter Weisz, my publisher

A Social Illusion

Special Thanks

I believe that people land in our lives for a reason. In 2019 I met Eric Kussin, founder and CEO of #SameHere – The Global Mental Health Movement. Eric has since become a friend and trusted advisor. He has provided me and countless others with a platform to give back and help normalize society's perceptions of mental health. Eric's 'stand together' approach is how we will make the topic of mental health as common as our physical health, and ultimately save lives. To find out more about Eric's inspirational story, visit samehereglobal.org.

About the Author

In 2019, Jason published his first book, *The Magic of Mayfair*, a coming-of-age memoir that helps readers overcome their own life challenges. In the story, Jason writes about navigating through the emotions of his brother's schizophrenia diagnosis and his childhood best friend's suicide. Today, Jason advocates in their honor to normalize society's perceptions of mental health and make it part of our everyday conversation.

Jason donates his time to #SameHere – The Global Mental Health Movement and works directly with the organization's founder, Eric Kussin. #SameHere believes mental health lives on a continuum ranging from "thriving" to "sinking" as a result of life's inevitable challenges.

In December of 2021, Jason founded the #SameHere Author's Alliance. This group of published authors believes that through literature we can connect society by the commonalities of challenges we all face.

To find out more about Jason, please visit his website: treemouth-books.com.

Made in United States
Orlando, FL
09 July 2022

19571630R00074